Return of the Calico Kids

By Todd Downing

FIRST EDITION

ISBN: 978-1-961545-03-8

Edited by Randy Hensel, Dan Heinrich & Raechelle Downing
Cover design by Todd Downing

WWW.TODDDOWNING.COM

Deep7 Press is a subsidiary of Despot Media, LLC
1214 Woods Rd SE Port Orchard, WA 98366 USA
WWW.DEEP7.COM

*To those who have discovered
the secret to growing older
without growing up*

Foreword

I didn't mean it.

When I released *Calico Kids* in 2020, I figured it to be a one-and-done, self-contained story. It was, after all, a snapshot of a very specific place and time, intended to evoke the emotions and (for those readers of a certain age) the sense memory of growing up unsupervised in a suburban or rural community.

The characters had resolved their conflicts and various arcs, the narrative was complete, and that was that—or so I thought.

When *Calico Kids* was written, it was a departure from my *Airship Daedalus* pulp adventure series. I'd seen it as a palate-cleanser, a momentary distraction, after which I would return to the AEGISverse. And I did.

But something else happened.

Calico Kids struck a nerve. I wasn't aware of how deeply at first, but over time it became apparent that folks were *really* enjoying the novel. It quickly became—and has remained—my top-selling and most favorably rated book.

Then readers started asking me when the sequel was coming.

Initially flustered, I would hand-wave such queries and offer lame excuses as to why there was no more story to tell. Not everything requires a sequel, after all.

But over time, I came to realize there was in fact more story to be found in the quaint retro-'80s setting. I had characters ascending through their teenage years, with all the changes and obstacles unique to adolescence. Hell, even the adult characters were interesting. It eventually became apparent that they weren't done with me yet.

And then I realized I'd conveniently left a loose thread in the first book. As I gently pulled on it, it revealed what I thought could be a fun and compelling premise for a fol-low-up.

So although I never originally intended *Calico Kids* to have a second volume, a strange confluence of reader inquiries, input from friends and fellow authors, and the simple act of *listening to the characters* has brought us here. Back to the sleepy riverside community in unincorporated Curry County, Oregon.

Welcome back to Calico.

A quick word of warning: this story follows the characters from the first book another year into the future—1984. They are older, and the themes are darker and a bit more mature. This was done deliberately to reflect how quickly we evolve in our teen years (and appropriate, considering the PG-13 rating was instituted in 1984).

Please enjoy *Return of the Calico Kids*.

- Todd Downing, Port Orchard, WA

Summer, 2024

A Few Things

Chapters are given a song title, along with the artist and year of release. Think of it as a mix-tape of sorts. The curated Spotify playlists can be found here:

www.todddowning.com/calico-kids

Immense gratitude to my readers.

Likewise, many thanks to Dan Heinrich, Trish Heinrich, Rob Lowry, Malcolm Collie, Julie Collie, Allan McComas, Raffael Boccamazzo, and Ron Dugdale, for beer and inspiration.

Tip of the hat to Mark Bruno and James Stubbs, who wrote the Boomtown Calico setting for my _Six Gun_ RPG.

Thanks also to my editing team and sounding boards: Randy Hensel, Raechelle Downing, and Dan Heinrich (again).

Babciu is a Polish term of endearment for grandmother and is roughly pronounced "bob-chew".

Content warning: substance use/abuse, science fiction horror elements, violence, death, occult & supernatural themes.

Track 1:
THE GATHERING

Killing Joke (1983)

The dragon's flesh parted as Grodwell Thunderbeard struck true with his mighty dwarven war axe, his battle cry echoing through the cavern. But to the venerable Stonewyrm, it was but a scratch.

Its great talon struck out at the dwarf attacker, pelting it away, and the warrior called Thunderbeard landed in a tangled heap against the cave wall.

Sister Faris of the Grey Order rushed to the dwarf's side, ready with a prayer of healing. If the dedicated warrior in their group was neutralized, they may as well surrender and become Stonewyrm's midnight snack. She was not about to let that happen.

Wysteria lowered the hood of her cloak, revealing the graceful features and tapered ears of her elfin heritage. Drawing upon her knowledge of the arcane arts, she performed a series of mystical gestures, and a swirling orb of energy began to grow and brighten before her. In an ancient language lost to all but the most learned of occult scholars, she spoke the chant, and with a final word sent the crackling mass at the fearsome dragon foe.

The creature writhed in agony as the energy cratered into its massive shoulder, a savage roar reverberating through the chamber. It circled toward the source of its pain, focusing large reptilian eyes on the sylvan mage. With a rumble that seemed to percolate from the very earth under its feet, Stonewyrm began to inhale.

Wysteria felt her face go white. The dragon was about to breathe fire.

"Stop, fiend!" came a shout in the high timbre of a halfling voice to the left. Skoot the thief was all of three feet in height, jolly face ringed in raven curls. He brandished an enchanted short sword in a calloused hand. "We will have your golden hoard, or we will have your life!"

The momentary distraction was enough for his companions to scramble a hasty exit, but the dragon's breath was taken, its lungs full. The fire had to be expelled.

With a colossal bellow, an irresistible cascade of blistering flame spewed from the monster's maw, vaporizing poor Skoot in a mere instant. As the halfling's sword fell red-hot to the floor of the cave, the dragon Stonewyrm withdrew to its sanctum, content to lick its wounds and fight another day.

☙

"That's not what happened!" Kris protested.

Golden sunset dimmed in the sky over Calico, Oregon. A small town nestled on the north bank of the Rogue River, just a shy couple of miles inland from the Pacific Ocean, Calico was home to a modest population of working-class folks who made a living in one of the two major local industries. Those who weren't employed by the salmon cannery or the pulp mill worked for one of the many businesses that supported them.

With summer creeping upon the rural town, the teenage children of those working-class adults would soon be seeking employment as well. And other diversions, besides.

Five such teenagers were gathered presently to listen to—and pronounce judgment on—the epic fantasy story they'd just heard.

A.J. groaned, gingerly closing the wire-bound notebook in his lap. "I know, but I had to take some creative license. It's just how this works." Alan Jenkins was fifteen and skinny, a wiry scarecrow with a mop of dishwater blond hair which hid an acne-pocked forehead. Brown eyes peered from behind thick lenses, and he crossed and uncrossed his legs nervously, the denim of his Levi's scraping quietly in the chair. "Makes more sense that Skoot makes a noble sacrifice at this point in the story."

Kris waved a dismissive hand. "Whatever. It's just not the way it went down."

Kristof Korolewski had just turned sixteen, and had sprouted over the past year. Now six-foot-two with a chiseled jaw, Kris had the rippling physique of a young man who cycled everywhere and bused tables at the family restaurant. His parents, immigrants from Poland, doted on him. They also expected him to work the family business during much of his non-school time.

"Don't be mad, pookie bear," consoled Molly with a face full of satirical concern. She was seated next to Kris on the basement rec room sofa, feet in his lap. A lithe, athletic girl of fifteen, Molly Reynolds prided herself on being the antithesis of the typical teenage girl. She eschewed the preppy fashion and teen magazine culture of her peers, opting instead for interests like videogames and horror movies, skater clothes, and *Dungeon & Dragons*. She kept her hair colorful, pulled into a ponytail that revealed a buzzed back and sides. Molly took most of her cultural cues—music and clothing included—from older brother Bodhi, currently on a backpacking jaunt through Europe while on summer break from UCLA.

The Reynolds parents ran their own real estate agency, and were often occupied with its operation. Thus Molly ruled the roost at home, especially when her friends gathered in the basement for shooting some pool, playing a *D&D* campaign, or watching rented movies on the VCR.

Kris wasn't having the patronizing display. "Whatever, *pookie bear*," he dismissed.

Chlöe let out a dramatic sigh and crossed her arms as she leaned against the pool table. Tall and poised in jeans and a light sweater, with a mane of styled blond hair, she looked far more adult than her actual seventeen years. Her tenure as a football cheerleader at Calico High School ("Go Lumberjacks!") had been cut short when she chose the ghost hunting activities of a certain group of nerds back in the fall of '82. "Well I liked it, A.J." Extending a hand to the green felt table top, she pushed the cue ball to bank off the padded bumper. It smacked into a cluster of stripes and solids. "As long as Sister Faris gets her XP for healing the dwarven dumbass..."

"Heal this," Liam muttered. Despite being a high school sophomore like Kris and A.J., he was mentally older than the other boys, owing to a troubled home life and equally troubled scholastic history. A tangle of dark hair and deep olive skin told of indigenous heritage— primarily Shasta and Coquille. He'd grown into his old Army jacket in the past year, still a slender frame of coiled muscle, but now more of it. "Yeah, yeah, artistic license. What I wanna know is, why you changed the name of my character in the story."

A.J. frowned, clamping his eyes shut in dismay. "Because 'Grodwell Thunderbeard' is a cool name for a dwarf in a fantasy story, and 'Codswell Thunderbutt' is not."

"Aww, come on, man! He's called 'Codswell' because of his massive—"

"Dude!" Molly interrupted, not bothering to look at him. "We know already! Jeez!"

Kris lolled his head on the back of the sofa, craning his neck to see Liam standing by the counter in the kitchenette. "And Thunderbutt because he can't help farting every five minutes...like you."

Liam loved getting under their skin. It was the last vestige of his old bullying behavior from junior high. *"Abso-fucking-lutely,"* he grinned, shifting his focus to A.J. "But when they make the movie, you're changing it back."

All eyes rolled, and A.J. took the ultimatum in stride. "I promise, Liam. If they ever make a movie adaptation of the *Raiders of Stonewyrm*, I will change his name back to Codswell Thunderbutt."

"Right on. Good story, otherwise," Liam shrugged.

Kris reached for his open can of root beer, nudging Molly's feet off his lap. "Yeah, I guess it's okay."

"I liked it," Chlöe repeated.

Molly shifted on the couch. "It's great, man, really coming along," she said, reaching over absentmindedly to rub circles on the small of Kris' back.

A.J. noticed, but said nothing. The two had been acting funny since Memorial Day weekend, when the group had gone to see *Indiana Jones and the Temple of Doom* at the Star theater in Port Orford together. But as much as A.J. wanted to know what was going on between two of his closest friends, he knew it was best if they got it sorted without anyone's intervention, no matter how well-intentioned.

"I'm gonna jet," Liam said, pushing away from the counter. "Last day of school tomorrow, boys and girls!"

Chlöe raised her hands as if at a prayer meeting. "Hallelujah," she sang.

"Dude, can I bum a ride?" A.J. was already standing, backpack in hand, before he finished the question. It was a perfunctory gesture, really. Liam and A.J. had an unspoken contract. A.J. threw a few bucks his way now and again for gas, and Liam ferried A.J. anywhere along his existing trajectory.

Liam cocked his head toward the stairwell, and started up to the main floor. *"Hasta mañana,"* he waved.

A.J. followed, Chlöe close behind him.

"See you guys tomorrow." She paused on the bottom step. "Kris, you need a lift home?"

Kris and Molly exchanged a look, and Kris shook his head. "That's okay, thanks. I'm gonna hang out awhile."

Chlöe pursed her lips, intrigued. "Okay, don't forget your yearbooks—I wanna leave some random, nasty notes in them. Stuff you won't find for a few years."

The moon began to rise above the Rogue River-Siskyou National Forest, a nearly-perfect silver orb peeking above the tree line, just two days from fullness. Liam went to the metallic black El Camino in the Reynolds' driveway, and A.J. hefted his Huffy BMX bike into its open bed. Chlöe waved at the boys as she ducked into her father's orange Toyota Corolla hatchback.

They wound down from North Bank Overlook to where North Bank Rogue River Road began, following the natural contour of the riverfront, past the high school campus and into the downtown area, what there was of it. Chlöe took a left at Cedar Street, heading back up the hill to her family home in the Cedar Heights neighborhood, while Liam and A.J. continued on the frontage, behind the warehouses by the pulp mill.

"Crazy we're gonna be juniors next year," A.J. said. "High school's half over."

Liam nodded, his mind clearly elsewhere. "Yup."

"I take it you noticed how weird Kris and Molly have been acting," A.J. offered.

Liam chuckled in a voice that had dropped long ago. "Dude, of course. Molly's had the hots for Kris since she first met him."

"Really?" A.J. shot back, honestly shocked at the news.

Liam nodded as he negotiated the turn up the road by the junior high school. "Duh."

"Well, okay then. Guess if it causes shit within the group, we'll burn that bridge when we come to it." A.J. paused amid the mixed metaphor, letting the late-spring evening breeze ruffle his hair through the open passenger window. "How's your mom doing?" he asked.

Liam was quiet for several seconds. Finally, he cleared his throat and muttered, "Hell if I know, man. I knew it was a bad idea to start waitressing at the saloon. Been coming home drunk almost every night." He pulled over at the T where Hill Avenue split from the frontage road, offering A.J. a short bicycle ride home, most of it downhill. "Not much I can really do about it, y'know?"

"Yeah," A.J. sighed. "Sorry, man."

Liam gave his passenger a soft punch in the shoulder. "Get home safe. See ya tomorrow."

A.J. smiled. "You too, buddy," he said, slamming the door shut and hauling the bike from the bed of the El Camino. He saddled up and pedaled into the darkening night as the truck rumbled away, with "Codswell Thunderbutt!" bellowing from the driver's side window —like a primal battle cry, complete with accompaniment by Iron Maiden on the cassette deck.

Track 2:
LONELY SIDE OF TOWN
Y&T (1983)

Liam cracked the front door to the small dwelling on the upper corner of West Evergreen Drive, a lonely assemblage of shabby homes on the outskirts of town. The Scott residence was actually among the nicer places on the street, which may have been damning with faint praise. A manufactured box from the mid-1960s, it had been badly in need of maintenance for almost as long. But at three bedrooms, it was larger than most nearby homes, and occupied the corner lot, giving Liam plenty of yard to dig holes or light fireworks in when he was growing up.

He stood momentarily silhouetted in the doorway, the interior dark and silent. His mom's primer-gray Volkswagen Dasher sat in the driveway. She was either home from her shift early, had called in sick, or was out with a new boyfriend. It was even money which case was true.

If it was a new boyfriend, he hoped she'd wait a minute before bringing him home. He'd witnessed a parade of potential stepdads wander through his young life, and precisely *one* of them had been worth a damn. Liam had actually taken a liking to her last steady boyfriend, Paul. The guy was an underwater welder, and showed Liam how to make his own bong with scraps from the garage. But one drunken bender after another had showed Paul the absolute lack of any practical future with Amber Scott, and he'd hit the road about five months ago.

He moved to the wall switch and flicked on the light, shutting the door behind him. Most families had a key hook or bowl for car keys and spare change by the front door, but Liam's keys went directly to his coat pocket. He knew from experience that if he left them out of his direct control, the car could very well end up in hock to pay off his mother's debts, or support her addictions. He loved his mom, of course, but he knew better than to trust her with the vehicle Eren had given him specifically. Not only was it a lovingly customized machine and memento of the most incredible human being he'd ever met, but it also represented freedom—or its promise, when high school was eventually behind him.

Just two more years.

If he could only hold it together.

He ambled into the kitchen and opened the fridge, grabbing a can of Coke from inside. His plan for the night was already coalescing in his mind. Retire to his room, open the window, roll a fat blunt, put a mix tape in the boombox, and enjoy the latest issue of either *Car & Driver* or *Penthouse*.

Padding as quietly as possible in well-worn Eddie Bauer hiking boots, Liam cracked the door to his mother's bedroom and peered into the dark. Amber Scott was asleep. He could see the rise and fall of her breathing, and the empty Wild Turkey bottle on the floor next to the bed told him she wouldn't be stirring any time soon.

He was free to spark up.

Quietly shutting the bedroom door, Liam made his way across the open living room to his ten-by-twelve fortress of solitude, and a hazy escape.

CR

Although regular class schedules were still in effect, both students and staff treated the last day of school as an open social event. Teens clustered in small groups across the high school campus, trading yearbooks back and forth, defacing the photos and filling the pages with "So glad we met this year!", "Stay cool!", and "Have a good summer!"

Liam pulled the El Camino into the parking lot and squinted through mirrored shades into the late morning sun. It was not at all surprising that he was late, and even less so that he didn't particularly care. No administrator wanted to assign detention on the last day of school, and no teacher wanted to stay and monitor the riffraff.

Coach Carlisle—big, bald and bronze—hailed him as he entered the main office, admiring his "pretty sweet ride." Liam smiled and leaned over the counter to greet Becky Marsh, the school secretary. She was perky and plump, strawberry hair in curls framing a freckled face. She checked the record sheet for his name, and found he had paid for his yearbook.

As she got up to retrieve a copy from the stack of boxes behind her, he caught sight of a poster for the D.A.R.E. program on the wall next to the principal's office. He was still chuckling about it when Becky returned with his annual. She chirped something about having a great summer, but he was already halfway out the door.

With his yearbook in hand, Liam strode the halls of Calico High School, searching for his adventuring party. Copies of the hardcover annual had just arrived earlier in the week, and he inhaled the fumes of freshly printed pages and bindery glue. A paltry high, but a free one.

He found the gang in the center quad, across from a congregation of jocks and their erstwhile cheerleader girlfriends. Kris and Molly sat on the wooden planter bench in much the same position as when he'd last seen them in the basement rec room. A.J. stood nearby, leg propped on the redwood planks next to them, scrawling a note in the open yearbook on his thigh. Liam scanned around for Chlöe, finally locating her as she extricated herself from a tense interaction with Scott Rankin, student body president and three-sport varsity letterman.

Kris noted Liam's arrival and nodded in his direction. "There he is. The man, the myth, the legend."

"Nice of you to join us," Molly chided.

Liam ignored the reference to his tardiness. He was used to it. Someday they'd realize that he just had no sense of urgency in relation to events he didn't care about, and school was one of those things. Now, ask him to catch a movie or pick you up at 5 a.m. for a camping trip and he was Johnny-on-the-spot. School, not so much.

He waved the hardcover annual in his hand. "Whose yearbook gets to be deflowered by me?"

"Uh, hate to break it to you," A.J. muttered, "but nobody here has a virgin yearbook."

Molly chuckled. "We've been signing all morning." She pursed her lips suggestively. "Over...and over...and over..."

Kris blushed, and Liam took particular notice of it. A.J. was right when he said he thought they'd been seeing each other. And doing more than "seeing", if he was correct. "Yeah, but nobody's had my hand in 'em," he winked, folding his sunglasses and hanging them on the stretched collar of a Van Halen T-shirt.

"Whoa, doctor!" A.J. blinked, closing the annual and passing it to Liam. "Here's Molly's. She's looking forward to having you write in her crack."

"Well now you've spoiled the joke." Liam traded Molly's book for his own, opening it to a relatively untouched page and scrawling in the inner margin: "Looks like I'm the first to write in your crack. You will never beat my high score on *Asteroids*. Have a great summer. Liam."

A.J. opened Liam's annual, inhaling a fresh bouquet of printing chemicals much as Liam had earlier. He flipped the pages to an open spread near the end, above the business card ads for Aldo's Pizza and Dave's Deli. Scribbling a note he thought hilarious now—but would have absolutely zero meaning to Liam's future self, A.J. nodded a greeting to Chlöe as she joined the gang.

"Well, that's over with," Chlöe sighed, more tired than sad.

Molly swung her legs from the bench so that her feet scuffed the pebbles in the aggregate concrete. "How'd he take it?"

"Like you'd expect," Chlöe replied, flipping radiant hair over her shoulder. "Played it off like no big deal, which is fine. I really don't need that drama. He just wanted to get into my jeans."

Liam laughed under his breath. "Nothing wrong with that."

Chlöe's eyes cartwheeled to the back of her head, and Molly scowled, "What's that supposed to mean?"

Liam sighed. "Aww come on. It's not a big deal. Bodhi's been in her jeans already."

Molly clenched her jaw, trying desperately to stop an angry tirade from bursting out.

"Yeah," Chlöe admitted, unwilling to rise to the bait. "Yeah, he has. And he was absolutely worth it."

Liam registered the looks of disapproval from the group, and he knew he'd over-stepped. "Sorry, Chlöe. I didn't mean—"

"It's cool," she waved off his apology. "I just can't wait for Bodhi to get back."

A.J. looked puzzled. "Isn't he already out for the summer?"

"He's hiking around Germany for a month," Molly shrugged. "Whatever. Not like *I* wanted to hike around Germany for a month."

Kris flashed a bright smile at her. "Yeah, but you've been to space!"

His earnest expression was adorable. It made her giddy.

"In another dimension!" Liam added.

A.J. raised an eyebrow at Chlöe. "That's probably why you get bored with most guys. Who can hold a candle to shooting alien drones in space?"

"Exactly," Kris agreed. "We got to live *Scooby Doo* and *Galaga* in one summer!"

Yearbooks continued circulating among the group, and A.J. took notice of the goth girl from his AP English Lit class sitting alone by the library entrance, snapping shots with a Nikon SLR camera. In the few interactions they'd had over the school year, he'd gathered she had an interest in photography, and considerable talent in the adjacent graphic arts. She seemed to like a lot of the bands he liked, judging by her collection of concert tees and notebook graffiti. That was cool and all, but he was also intrigued by her furtive Asian features and dark fashion sense. In a town full of white kids, blue jeans and country music, that made her stand out.

He figured she would probably make a fine addition to the group, if he ever got up the courage to invite her in.

Kris finished writing in Chlöe's yearbook and passed it along. "You guys think it's true about Halverson?"

Chlöe frowned. "What's true about Halverson?"

"Are you kidding?" Kris shot back, suddenly animated. "You haven't heard the rumors?"

A.J. cleared his throat. "Kris, you've been one of those old town gossips since we were in third grade. No, we haven't heard the rumors."

Kris straightened, suddenly flush with the power he felt whenever he was able to share some morsel of information unknown to the rest of the group. "Some of the kids in Mrs. Bond's history class were saying he got caught up in something pretty ugly."

"Like what?" Liam offered. "Your undies?"

Kris ignored him. "Like underage girls."

"Unlikely," Chlöe scoffed. "At least no one I know."

"Yeah, but Curry County isn't just Calico, y'know." Kris leaned forward on the bench. "You don't know everyone."

Liam grunted, finishing with Chlöe's yearbook. "Not buyin' it, dude." He handed it over, and she began perusing the messages within.

"Agreed," said A.J. as he passed a book to Molly, stealing a glance at the goth girl across the quad and disappointed to find her gone. "Halverson's a total boy scout. Doesn't add up."

Kris looked at his old friend, deflated. "Wow, man. Not used to you shooting down a juicy rumor."

"I shoot down juicy rumors all the time."

"Like the Satanists in the forest?"

A.J. started to stammer something, then recovered. "You...that's not...that wasn't just casual gossip. The cops actually thought those kids in '72 might have been kidnapped by cult members."

Kris stood, folding recently buff arms across his chest. "You thought that's what happened to Jeannie Wells and Eric Somerville."

"Dude," A.J. huffed, shaking his head in disbelief. "That was just a working theory. *Before* we found out about the sigils and Eren and all that stuff."

"He's right," Molly stated matter-of-factly. "Apples and oranges."

Chlöe let out a sound of frustration that was a cross between a grunt and the air brakes on a Mack truck. "Goddamnit, Liam! You know the umlaut goes over the O."

In almost two years of friendship, Liam had never been able to remember which vowel in her name was accented. Most of the Chloës and Zoës he knew of had the dots above the E at the end. He shrugged helplessly. "Your parents spelled your name funny."

Kris frowned, still on topic. "I don't think it's far-fetched. You remember the sheriff before Chavez..."

"The sheriff before Chavez was a racist piece of shit," A.J. said.

Liam nodded in agreement. "And a rapist, turns out."

"Yeah," Chlöe sighed. "We all know Halverson. He's a straight arrow."

Kris gave a laugh of quiet contempt. "They're always the ones who turn out to have bones buried in the yard and lampshades made of human skin."

A.J. had to laugh. Kris wasn't wrong. Despite his doubts, A.J. had nothing to gain in defending Pete Halverson. Odds were good that this rumor would dissipate over the summer, like ninety-nine percent of all unfounded rumors. If there was anything to it, they'd all find out sooner or later. It wasn't really anyone's business, least of all theirs.

"We playing tonight?" Kris wondered.

A.J. cracked a half smile. The guy truly had the attention span of a hamster, and it was usually a fun time to be along for the ride.

"Yeah," Liam sighed, finishing a raunchy drawing next to the Silver City Diner ad in the back of Kris' yearbook. "But first we gotta see if Molly can crack the top three on *Tempest*."

Chlöe shrugged. "A burger sounds good, I guess. Meet at the diner?"

"After school," A.J. nodded. "I wanna have enough time afterward to finish the campaign." He arched his eyebrows maniacally, adding, "And kill you all."

Track 3:

HOME BY THE SEA

Genesis (1983)

The Silver City Diner was alive with the specific brand of energy that comes from teenagers on summer break. Unbridled chaos crackled from every booth and table as fries, cheeseburgers, and thick chocolate milkshakes were consumed. The place had been packed since the early bell released the high schoolers from their learning obligations. The diner filled first, due to its close proximity to Calico High. When it reached capacity, Mama's Deli, Aldo's Pizza, and the 1st Avenue Grill would be next in line, with the handful of tiny cafés and the ice cream shop filling in the gaps. The A&W on Pioneer Avenue would also be packed.

The last day of school was a good time to be a food vendor in Calico.

Kris donned a knee-length blue apron, ferrying plates to and fro as Molly steadily climbed the roster of high scores on the *Tempest* machine in the tiny arcade alcove. Liam, Chlöe and A.J. shared their customary family booth in the center of the dining room, surveying their domain over empty plates and plastic cups half-full of soda.

A.J. watched as Deputy Halverson sat hunched at the bar, burger untouched. His Sheriff's Department ball cap was pulled low on his brow. Eyes sunken. Face unshaven. He'd lost weight over the past year, and was clearly in a state of fatigue. Or depression.

As the boisterous hum of teen excitement swirled around him, the deputy slowly rose from his stool and tossed a couple of crinkled fives on the counter. He strode from the restaurant, unsmiling, detached from any attempt at human interaction.

The police Bronco rumbled to life and turned out of the small parking lot, and A.J. thought for the first time that Kris might have been onto something with his earlier gossip. He exchanged a silent look with Liam, as Chlöe chattered on about planned activities once Bodhi returned home. Camping out by Hanging Rock, fishing in Agness, road trips up the coast to Florence, or over to Eugene. Apparently this summer was to be one incredible outdoor adventure after another, especially since there was a third licensed driver in the group. And Bodhi, now nineteen, could get the under-seventeens into rated-R movies now.

A.J. glanced up from his empty plate to catch the briefest moment of eye contact with the goth photographer from school before she returned her attention to the magazine in front of her, delicately swirling the straw in her drink. She sat alone at one of those awkward tables for two that every restaurant had.

Shit, what is her name? A.J. thought, wracking his brain for clues from the past school year. *Lisa? Lizzie? Laura?* He would definitely have to strike up a conversation with her. Eventually.

One of these days.

∝

Pete Halverson entered the Sheriff's Headquarters in Gold Beach at 3:30 p.m., the tiny office bustling with activity. With the end of the school year came an immediate uptick in petty crimes like vandalism and disorderly conduct. Minor offenses were usually met with a reprimand and parental phone call, while the more serious cases could end up in front of a judge. And of course there would be the usual surge in underage drinking, coupled with more driver's licenses issued—not an ideal combination.

Halverson took it as given that before the end of summer, he'd be scraping at least one local teen off the asphalt of US 101.

The chatter of conversations and the electronic ring of incoming telephone calls swirled around him as he made his way through the office.

A large form loomed up in his path, and Halverson had an immediate flashback to his high school football career. Mike Lewis topped out at six-foot-three, with coils of muscle and a shaved head. His bronze skin was definitely out of place in a state which had been founded on the exclusion of his kind. But Sheriff Chavez wasn't about to carry on that particular tradition, especially when presented with such an exemplary candidate as Lewis. He'd come out to the Oregon coast from the community of Weed, a lumber town in Northern California that had been largely populated by Italian immigrants at the turn of the century, followed by an influx of black mill workers from Louisiana in the 1920s.

"Mike," Halverson nodded, preparing to step around the new deputy.

Lewis returned the nod, gesturing toward the sheriff's office with a thumb. "Chavez wanted to see you when you came in."

Halverson paused in his tracks, glancing around the busy office with nervous intensity. "Shit."

"Hey man," Lewis replied, raising his hands in front of a toned chest, "I'm just the messenger." He moved aside and continued to the water cooler.

Halverson took a deep breath and proceeded to the office door with SHERIFF LINDA CHAVEZ painted on the glass in gold lettering shadowed in black. The sheriff had seen his approach through the aluminum blinds and stood from behind the desk as he entered. She was short woman with a solid, muscular frame that was also curvaceous somehow. She looked like someone had packed too much chorizo into a sausage casing that was too small.

"Ah, Pete. Come in. Have a seat."

Halverson removed his hat and lowered his gaze to the floor. "Thanks, I'm good."

Chavez paused, new lines around her eyes and mouth evident in the fluorescent light of the office. The past couple years serving Curry County had put exponentially more wear on her body than any other posting. But she loved her job. Lived for it, really. "Pete," she began softly, "we can't ignore this anymore. This heat is coming from the federal level."

Halverson slumped his shoulders, refusing to meet her eyes. "I didn't...these accusations...they're trying to get me to stop looking into—"

"Yes, I know. They're bullshit. I believe you. You *know* I believe you."

"I know."

"You know I back you," she offered.

"I know."

Chavez frowned in obvious discomfort. "But until we can get to the bottom of this, I'm gonna have to put you on suspension."

He caught her gaze with a look of silent desperation, then his eyes fell again toward the floor. "Yeah," he sighed. "Yeah, that sounds about right."

Chavez approached, dwarfed by the larger man. She placed a friendly hand on his shoulder. "Go home, Pete. Let us work on this. If you're being honest with me, I'm sure this will turn out to be nothing."

Halverson exhaled, visibly deflating, broken. "Sure," he said quietly. "You know where to find me." Then he turned and left the office, heading for the afternoon sunshine outside.

Sheriff Chavez leaned against her desk and clenched her jaw. She'd get to the bottom of this. She had to. Not just for Halverson, but for the sake of her whole department.

‽

The die was cast.

A red plastic polyhedral clattered to the center of the hand-drawn map on the coffee table, rolling to a stop with the 20 face showing. The basement rec room erupted with cheers.

"Natural twenty!" Molly exclaimed, pumping her fist in the air.

A.J. sighed, exhausted. Molly had rolled at least three natural 20s during this game session alone, which ordinarily would have made A.J. suspicious of the die she was using, except she'd been rolling dice from Kris' bag— dice that he and A.J. had used since they first picked up the hobby in the sixth grade.

They'd *never* rolled this well for Kris.

"Okay, and that was a called shot, right?"

"Yep," Molly grinned. "Arrow to the face, baby!"

Kris chuckled. "Epic."

"Let's see. The ogre was already down to minimal hit points. Not sure you even need to roll damage here." A.J. consulted his notes and saw that even the smallest damage result would dispatch the creature. "Your well-aimed arrow flies from your bow and pierces the ogre's left eye, exiting through the back of its skull, taking chunks of brain matter with it. It falls dead to the ground."

Liam grinned from ear to ear. "Totally *moist!*"

"Ewww!" Chlöe protested. "You know I hate that word!"

Kris shrugged. "I'd say 'moist' is pretty accurate, really."

"Staaaahp!" Chlöe scolded, squirming on the old sofa.

There was a momentary pause, then everyone chimed in about the topic, and agreed, to Chlöe's supreme horror, that given the blood and viscera, "moist" was indeed the correct technical description of the episode. It was in fact the *most* moist—the *moistest*, Molly insisted.

A.J. doled out experience points for each character, noting the subtle, unspoken interactions between Molly and Kris. The way she placed a gentle hand on his leg while reaching for her pencil, the way Kris smiled when he caught a whiff of her hair as she leaned forward.

"So we saved the kingdom," Liam said. "What next?"

A.J. shrugged. "You took out the ogre, rescued the Lord Mayor's daughter, and retrieved the stolen gems. That's pretty much the end of the campaign. "

Kris cleared his throat. "We could try this game I found at that place in Grant's Pass. *Traveller*. It's sci-fi..."

"Not *that*," Molly scoffed. "I don't wanna play a game where you can die during character creation."

A.J. held up a hand. "Yeah, but it doesn't happen all that often, and you gotta admit it creates higher emotional stakes."

"Speaking of emotional stakes," Liam smirked, "you gonna ask that vampire girl out?"

A.J. deflected with some word salad about how busy he'd be, working at the drug store, saving some money, etcetera. Liam knew he'd hit a nerve.

Chlöe sipped from a can of Sprite and shot a look at Liam, trying to redirect the conversation. "You got any plans for the summer?"

"I'll be part-time at the auto shop," he said, referring to Gary's Auto Shop, the place Eren had first spotted the El Camino he now drove. "But tonight, I'm gonna go to my favorite spot on the river to smoke a joint and watch the meteor shower. Everyone's welcome, but if you want to share my weed, you're chipping in."

A.J. and Kris had tried it enough to know that smoking pot wasn't for them, but Liam didn't pressure them, and in return, they didn't hassle him about it. Apparently it didn't affect his work performance at the garage, so live and let live.

"Nah, thanks," A.J. declined, noticing how Kris and Molly were leaning closer on the sofa next to Chlöe. "I actually have a shift tomorrow. And when your mom's your manager..."

Kris nodded. "Tell me about it."

"Your *mom's* your manager," Molly giggled, making a "your mom" joke out of a literal statement of fact.

"So let's play it by ear," A.J. said. "If anyone throws together a game, I'm most likely in."

"Killer." Kris began gathering up the dice strewn across the coffee table and putting them into the velvet Crown Royal bag he'd procured from his dad.

Liam stood and thrust his character sheet and dice haphazardly into his backpack. It was why they always looked like they'd been fished out of a garbage can. "Okay then. It's getting dark. I'm gonna head home and get a start on tonight's festivities."

"Hey," A.J. began, zipping up his own backpack. "Can I—"

Liam tiredly craned his neck toward the basement stairwell. "Come on."

With the latest *D&D* campaign over and school out, it really felt like a threshold had been crossed. Like summer was truly here, even though the actual solstice was still more than a week away. The friends said goodnight at Molly's front door, and once again Kris remained behind.

It was beyond obvious now, though no one mentioned it.

As Chlöe went her way in the family station wagon, Liam and A.J. took a circuitous route through the streets of Calico. They hung a left onto North Rogue Drive as it wound alongside a small tributary of the river between the high school and elementary school. Taking a right on Pioneer Avenue, they jogged over onto 3rd, passing the Val-U Drug on the right. A.J. had requested the drive-by to see if his mom was still at work, but her car was gone. The only vehicle in the parking lot was a lone Ford Bronco with a Curry County Sheriff's Department insignia on the door.

Liam accelerated toward the turn at Lamont to get A.J. home.

Inside the truck, Deputy Pete Halverson thumbed through a manila file folder, illuminated by the single dome light in the cab.

45

Track 4:
SKETCH FOR SUMMER
Durutti Column (1980)

The Val-U-Drug on 3rd Avenue was as bland beige suburbia as it could possibly be, with its rows of greeting cards, crappy plastic toys, basic office supplies, and knick knacks fawned over by the older folks in the community. It did have a single pharmacist, Lydia Duffy, in her white lab coat, enormous tortoise shell glasses and auburn perm.

A.J. worked a part-time opening shift, 8 a.m. to noon. Sometimes 10 to 2. Having a manager who was also his mother was a double-edged sword. He couldn't get away with anything, but he also usually got his choice of hours. He also got to work the photo printer, something the drug store had added within the last couple of years. Before that, customers had to put their film in a yellow and white Kodak envelope and deposit it through a slot in the kiosk at the back of the store. If they were lucky, they might have their pictures back in a week. The self-contained Noritsu minilab behind the photo counter meant they could offer one-hour processing.

The sound of a customer clearing her throat startled A.J., who quickly stashed the bottle of developer he'd been feeding into the minilab's tank. Turning to the counter, he was met with the smiling face of the quiet goth photographer, untamed spray of jet black hair framing pale features. "Oh! Hey!" he stammered in a facsimile of recognition. "English Lit? You transferred in from...where was it?"

The girl nodded, a warm pink tint beginning to wash over her face and neck. "Yeah! From Stewart's Cove. It's...A.J., right?"

"It's Alan, but yeah," he blushed in kind. "A.J. is what my friends call me. That, or dumbass."

"I highly doubt that," she laughed. "Not the dude who aced the Edgar Allan Poe exam."

A.J. shrugged. "What can I say? I know my mid-19th century angst."

"My man." The girl pursed her lips and offered her hand. "Name's Linh Tran, but I go by Lori."

He stood like a woodland creature caught in the beam of headlights from an oncoming car. She smelled like clove cigarettes and Dove soap, and he never wanted to move from that spot.

"Cool," he replied finally, giving her hand a brief shake. "What can I do for you?"

Lori paused, her mouth transforming from a thoughtful bow into a cocky half-smile. "What can you do for me?" she pondered dramatically. "What can you do...for me?"

A.J. flushed dark red. He felt his face sunburning in real time. "Um, I mean...um..."

"You can do two things for me," Lori said finally, breaking some of the enormous tension across the counter. "First, you can process this." She placed a canister of 35-millimeter film on the glass and pushed it toward him.

At the very least, he now had a task to distract him from the hormones flooding his adolescent brain. He was glad of both the counter between them and of the utility apron's coverage. "Sure," he sighed, pulling an empty photo envelope from a nearby cubby. "Is that L-A-U-R—?"

"L-O-R-I, actually."

A.J.'s head was swimming and he wasn't quite sure where he was. He watched his own hand scrawl the name *LORI* on the envelope. Suddenly the blood returned to his brain and he cleared his throat casually like he hadn't just taken a brief trip to outer space. "There's no other jobs ahead of you, so it'll just be about an hour." He slid the envelope under the film canister and pushed them both aside. "And what's the second thing?"

"Tell me your favorite band."

A.J. paused. "My favorite...?"

"Your favorite band."

"No, I heard you I just...absolute favorite?"

"Uh huh. There's a lot riding on this, so think about what you're gonna say."

Even for a kid who was often flustered, his reaction was extreme. Between the girl's intoxicating scent and the ominous undertone in her banter, he was drawing a complete blank. "I...don't have a favorite band," he said quickly, stalling for time.

Lori cocked her head, intrigued. "Explain?"

A.J. pivoted to his improvisational skills, honed through years of roleplaying games. "I mean, how do you choose between The Clash and The Pretenders? Between Siouxsie and The Cure? Chameleons or Cocteau Twins? Bauhaus or Joy Division? They all fit various moods, they all have their time and place. I love them too much to paint myself into a corner."

Lori regarded him for several seconds before the smile returned fully. "Good answer. Bonus points for mentioning Cocteau Twins.

Not many folks around here know them. You pass."

"Oh good," A.J. huffed, actually somewhat relieved. "What did I win?"

She winked, pushing away from the counter. "A future opportunity for more scintillating conversation with yours truly."

He watched her as she strode from the store, passing Liam as he entered.

"I look forward to it," A.J. muttered under his breath as he buttoned up the minilab and began preparing to run the film. His mouth suddenly felt very dry.

"Dude, were you actually talking to the goth chick?" Liam chuckled with an extra helping of snark. "Right on!"

A.J. rolled his eyes. "She was just dropping off a roll of film, and we got to talking about music."

"Yeah? I bet she likes that dirgy Bauhaus stuff."

"Dude, *you* like Bauhaus."

Liam nodded. "Damn straight. And I'm gonna go into Gold Beach and see if Pacific Records has their live album. It's import only. Maybe grab lunch at Gizmo's."

"You want company?" A.J. asked. "I'm off in about fifteen."

Liam shot a grin in his direction. "As if I'd waste my time in this seventh level of hell if I didn't want you to tag along." He pointed a finger-gun at A.J. and backed toward the greeting card aisle. "I'm gonna go chat up your mom while I'm waiting. Maybe ask her out."

It was Liam's way, to push the envelope of decorum just a few millimeters short of too far. A.J. knew he didn't mean anything by it, and therefore played along.

"Oh gawd," he grunted, powering up the photo processor. "She's a married woman!"

Liam flashed a heavy metal horns gesture and bared his tongue. "Not for long!"

☙

A.J. and Liam piled into the El Camino and headed out of the one-horse town of Calico, prowling toward the Wedderburn Bridge and the two-horse town of Gold Beach. *Actually,* A.J. thought, *Gold Beach might have TWO horses...and a WAGON.*

As they meandered up the two-lane country road that was State Route 545, the mouth of the Rogue came into view, usually clear of marine traffic this time of day. But as they met Highway 101 and turned south across the iconic bridge, they noticed some commotion below and to the west. A man-made breakwater where the river met the Pacific Ocean provided a shallow harbor for fishing charters and water scooter rental services, and one such boat was blocked in by a Coast Guard patrol craft and a runabout belonging to the Curry County Sheriff's Department, hazard lights blazing.

"Whoa," Liam grunted. "What's going on down there at Talbot's?"

A.J. shrugged, squinting from the passenger side window. Liam referred to Talbot Pacific Fishing Charters, a family business owned by Larry and Sue Talbot, third-generation residents of Curry County. As far as anyone knew, the Talbots had a sterling reputation and had never had any kind of trouble with the law. So seeing one of their boats crawling with cops of any variety gave them pause.

They couldn't stop on the bridge, and Liam wouldn't have wanted to if he could—there was a Bauhaus import with his name on it waiting at the record store. As was the case in any small community, the news would come out in due course, in the evening papers and local Coos Bay newscast later that night. But knowing that would do little to stanch the flood of gossip.

Liam found a convenient parking space between Gizmo's and the record store, angling in as the engine rumbled to a stop. On any Wednesday during the school year, Pacific Records resembled a ghost town inside, with the occasional retiree or tourist browsing the used bins for vintage Brubeck or Grateful Dead. But summer meant an influx of travelers and students with jobs, disposable income, and a hefty music habit.

A.J. went to the "New Wave" bins and began searching for anything that had arrived in the last month. He found copies of R.E.M.'s *Reckoning* and the second Meat Puppets album, while Liam scored his import of the Bauhaus live record, *Press the Eject and Give Me the Tape.*

The place was bustling, shoppers abuzz with an elevated energy that both boys couldn't help but notice. Rumors in hushed tones whirled around them as they flipped through the import bins, trying to ignore the various half-conversations. A.J. discovered a single-sided pressing of *Yello Live at the Roxy* and added it to his stack.

Eager to get clear of the ever present game of telephone, the boys paid for their records and headed down the block to Gizmo's Arcade & Pizza, their go-to summer hangout. Over slices of pepperoni and waxed paper cups of root beer, they compared their musical purchases, poring over the cover graphics and liner notes inside.

But the human grapevine soon followed as another group of Calico High students found their way to a nearby table, discussing the situation down at Talbot's, in animated fashion and at a volume impossible to ignore. The music and sound effects from the game cabinets were an 8-bit symphony, but even that couldn't drown out the Hearsay Machine.

According to the rumor mill at the next table, one of the Talbot charters had been leaving early that morning when something fouled its propeller.

It was a body.

Exactly whose body was not known. Only that someone had been drifting near the mouth of the Rogue River, and a fishing boat had run into said someone—and over them. Had they been alive prior to contact with the trawler? Unknown. Was it one of the many seasonal hired hands who'd maybe gotten drunk and fallen overboard? Possible. Had Sue Talbot really had a nervous breakdown in reaction to the grisly event, and been taken to Curry General for treatment? Not outside the realm of possibility. Unhinged speculation circulated like a case of the flu, and finally A.J. could stand no more.

On their way to the El Camino parked outside, A.J. realized Liam hadn't said a word for the past twenty minutes, and he wouldn't say anything at all for the duration of the drive home. His face was that of a mannequin, expressionless and unmoving, with the tight line of a mouth clamped shut. No nerdy banter. No quips, no dirty jokes or lame media references.

This was the first time A.J. could recall his friend acting in such a way. Liam was usually the life of the party. But it seemed like the community's grim discovery was really affecting him on a personal level, and A.J. knew he shouldn't pry, beyond a simple, "you okay, man?" which was answered with a simple grunt.

As they headed off the Wedderburn Bridge back into Calico, A.J. frowned at the figurative storm cloud gathering over his friend's countenance, bracing for the darkness to come.

Track 5:

GHOSTS ON THE ROAD

Guadalcanal Diary (1984)

Two empty pizza boxes lay open on the counter, devoid of contents except a few crumbles of Italian sausage and some petrified cheese.

The Reynolds' basement should have been alight with exuberant teen energy on summer break. It was, after all, a night for plotting the next roleplaying adventures, campouts, fishing excursions up the Rogue, and devouring Kris' latest haul from the new video rental store on Pioneer Avenue. But something was off. The energy was...weird somehow. The snarky banter which was usually in earnest seemed forced, performative. Each seemed to be in their own head.

Everyone except Kris. There was no forcing, no facade with that boy. He was a very what-you-see-is-what-you-get type of person.

And now that the group had thoroughly demolished a couple of pies from Aldo's, the visual entertainment could begin. Entertainment that he had volunteered to be responsible for.

"Okay, listen up, maggots," he said, fanning a selection of VHS tapes in front of him as if displaying a deck of cards in a magic trick. Each was housed in an identical plastic clamshell case with a Silver City Video label that included the movie title and year of release, along with a separate sticker which read: BE KIND - REWIND. "It's time to make your selection. We've got *Hawk the Slayer, Dragonslayer...*"

Molly chuckled. "All the slayers."

"What's with the slaying?" Chlöe wondered aloud.

Kris cleared his throat and continued, undeterred. "*Clash of the Titans,* or *Quest for Fire.*"

Liam pondered, tapping a finger on his scraggly chin. "That's the one where Tommy Chong's daughter invents the blowjob?"

Chlöe made a face, and A.J. gave a vague nod. "Yes. Yes it is."

"I vote that one," Liam decided.

"You would," Chlöe snorted. "Perv."

Liam bristled, "Hey, I didn't pick the rentals, Your Highnessness. Jesus, three of them show boobs." Then he added, "Not that I have a problem with that."

Chlöe was defiant. "That's lame. It's always boobs. Why don't they show any wang?"

"Because I think the MPAA considers that porn," Liam explained. Chlöe shot him an incendiary look, and he put up his hands in mock surrender. "I don't make the rules."

Kris shrugged, offering his best suggestion. "If you want wang, we could watch *Superman*."

"*Superman* doesn't show wang," Chlöe scoffed.

"Baby Kal-El," A.J. said, lazily thumbing through his hardcover *Dungeon Master's Guide*.

Molly nodded. "It's true. There's like three whole seconds of alien toddler peen."

"I'm not comfortable with this conversation, guys." Chlöe fumed, folding her arms across her chest with a pout.

A.J. held up a finger to draw her attention and make an official ruling. "Ahem. You were the one who wanted to see some wang."

"I didn't...but...you know what I..." Chlöe sputtered, finally composing herself along with a coherent sentence. "So which one doesn't have boobs?"

The selection had been made. Kris gave a deferential bow, pulling one videocassette from the group and setting the other three on the coffee table. "*Hawk the Slayer* it is."

"Are we not going to talk about the next campaign?" A.J. asked.

Molly sighed in disgust, scooting away from the pool table and heading to the kitchenette for a can of soda. "Are we not going to talk about the eight-headed mutant hydra in the room?"

Liam feigned shock. "That is a hell of a way to talk about your boyfriend."

Everyone froze in place as silence suddenly overtook the group. Granted, they all knew about Molly and Kris. At the very least, they suspected. But until now, nobody had dared address it. Liam had put words to an abstract concept. He'd actually said it, brought it into being.

It was now real.

Kris shifted his weight nervously from side to side, eyes downcast.

Molly paused dramatically, popping the tab on her can of Coke, which made everyone jump. "You know."

A.J. continued perusing the treasure tables in his book, not making eye contact. "Of course we know. We've known for a month."

Chlöe winced. "Maybe two."

After another few seconds of awkward silence, A.J. added, "It's totally cool, you guys."

Molly and Kris exchanged a look, breathing a unified sigh of relief.

"Really?" Kris asked, bracing for a change of heart from the group.

Liam smiled for the first time that day. "Really, dude."

"We didn't want it to be weird for the group," Molly explained.

"The only thing making it weird," A.J. countered, "was you two pretending that you're not a couple. Really, it's cool."

"Yeah," Chlöe agreed. "If you guys like each other, go for it. What kind of friends would we be if we got in your way?"

Liam pointed in her direction. "See? If the first inter-group dater says it's okay…"

Chlöe propped her hands on her hips and sneered at him. "Um, Bodhi and I were dating *before* I started hanging out with you guys."

"Yeah, but you're still, like, together, right? And Molly and Kris are together now, and A.J. actually talked to that goth girl today…"

"Wait, what?" Molly queried, delighted to have the spotlight thrust onto someone else for the moment. "What's this?"

A.J. started to speak, but was cut off by outbursts of, "no way!" and "you dog!"

"We haven't gone out or anything," he protested.

"Oh, it's coming," Liam assured him.

Now it was A.J.'s turn to shun the spotlight, so he closed the book with a pronounced *thump,* meeting Molly's eyes. "What was the eight-headed mutant hydra you were talking about?"

Molly took a sip of Coke and exhaled softly. "Duh. You didn't hear? They found Pete Halverson's body tangled up on one of Talbot's charters. Anchor line, or something."

The atmosphere in the rec room became noticeably, almost tangibly darker.

"Are you sure?" A.J. asked. "Where did you get that information?"

Molly nodded sadly. "Your uncle—the mayor—ran into my mom at the bank. I know it's secondhand info, but they found his rowboat drifting near the mouth of the river, by Talbot's breakwater..."

"Yeah..." A.J. slumped in the chair, recalling the last time he'd seen Halverson alive, hunched over his stool at the diner, looking besieged. "God, if we'd known..." He glanced across the room at Liam, who stared into distant space with a grim expression.

"I knew it," Liam muttered.

Kris frowned, confused. "What? You knew it was him?"

Thoughts began to coalesce in A.J.'s mind. Seemingly disparate elements that now began to take form. It wasn't that Liam had a close relationship with Deputy Halverson—quite the contrary. Liam reveled in his ability to get under the deputy's skin by addressing him on first name terms. And Halverson took every opportunity to ride Liam about the smallest of civil infractions. It was not inaccurate to say that they *almost* detested one another. So why had Liam been so closed off and miserable that afternoon as they browsed the record bins? It was almost certain that Liam knew more than he was sharing.

"We saw the cops at Talbots as we were going over the bridge into Gold Beach today," A.J. explained. "But we didn't find out who—"

"I'm not feeling too good, you guys," Liam interrupted. "Think I'm gonna jet. A.J., if you need a lift, let's go."

Chlöe reached toward him, concerned. "You okay?"

"I'm fine," he snapped, shrinking from her touch. "I just need to go."

A.J. stood and began collecting his belongings into the worn backpack at his feet. "Dude, yeah, of course. Sorry, guys. You go ahead and watch the movie without us, and we'll talk campaign next time."

Without further conversation, A.J. zipped the backpack and followed Liam up the stairs to the main floor, leaving Kris, Molly, and Chlöe more than a little somber and confused.

ભ

Liam dropped A.J. in front of his parents' carport, the El Camino roaring as he sped away. A.J. stood in the bleak evening breeze, eyes following the tail lights of the retreating car. It pulled out of sight at the ninety-degree bend in Ash Street, leaving the semi-rural block quiet and eerily still.

He had just turned away from the street to make his way inside when something shimmered in his periphery. A.J. turned slowly, trying to keep his heart from pounding through his chest. They hadn't seen a phantom in more than a year, not since Eren's departure. Not since they learned that interdimensional travel weakened the fabric of space-time, allowing entities from other realms—spirit realms—to wander through.

Yet here was a ghostly figure, a woman in Victorian dress, pale and translucent. She looked to be in her twenties, lithe and beautiful, with her hair pinned in a large bun. Sadness cut her cheeks with glistening tears.

A.J. pondered the life she must have led, living out here in that era—a century past—and what tragic fate must have befallen her. It could have been any number of factors, from disease to malnutrition, wild animals, childbirth, or rightfully angry natives. And that didn't count what old-timey coroners used to call "death by misadventure". Simply put, an accident.

Emitting an unearthly blue-white glow, the phantom wafted lazily up the road, directly toward him. It had been long enough since his last supernatural encounter that any desensitization was gone. His mouth lost all moisture immediately, and try as he might, he could not swallow. He hadn't had one of Grandma Korolewski's "special" pumpkin cookies, which allowed the eater to see spectral energy. This phantom was strong enough to be seen with the naked eye.

He recalled the first night they explored Old Town after dark, and the line of ghosts moving from the mouth of the old mine into the middle of town before disappearing. And then Halloween, when they'd ventured up the hill to the old McCabe mansion to close a ley line nexus spewing an endless parade of specters into town. He remembered a ghost possessing the local transient, and how they expelled the spirit with a solution of white vinegar and sea salt. He wasn't bothered so much by the dimensional travel, and fighting alien marauders in an alternate universe, but he'd never really gotten used to dealing with phantoms. They were shadows of the past, yet very present, and possible threats. It unnerved the hell out of him.

A.J. stood rooted in place, hoping the ghost would take no notice of him, though his blood thrummed in his eardrums, and he was sure his breathing could be heard clear down to the riverfront. As the specter glided past, toward the end of the block, she turned a pale head to gaze at him, her eyes a picture of pain long forgotten. But instead of approaching closer, she turned away, drifting toward the trees where she flickered like an old silent movie and disappeared.

Okay, what the hell?

A.J. watched the empty space where the ghostly woman had vanished. *Deputy Halverson turns up dead, and some random Victorian phantom—the first one sighted in a year— just cruises past my house, bright enough to see without the spirit cookies.*

Had one of the group been using the portals around Old Town? No one had used the sigil on his bedroom floor to teleport, that much he knew. Something weird was definitely going on, and as he stood vigil on the darkened street, he promised himself he would get to the bottom of it, whatever it was.

No matter how much it terrified him.

Track 6:
NIGHTMARES
A Flock of Seagulls (1983)

L iam arrived home to find the house he shared with his mother empty and dark. Not unexpected at 8 p.m., and not entirely un-welcome, the way his mom had been circling the drain of her alcoholism. The issue was further complicated by her job, serving drinks to the reprobates at Leo's Tavern.

He closed the front door, thinking the same thing he did every time he walked into that house: just two more years.

Out of sheer habit, he shuffled to the kitchen and opened the fridge, grabbing a can of Coke from the nearly empty space within. He leaned against the chipped counter and popped open the can, pausing at the sound of a car in the driveway outside. Turning to peer through the window above the sink, he could see a brown and white Bronco belonging to the Curry County Sheriff's Department, with its roof-mounted light bar—dark for the moment—and Sheriff Chavez bracing his mom as she guided her to the door.

Liam let out a tired sigh and set the soda can on the counter to open the front door for the two women.

"Sheriff," he nodded, gesturing into the living room.

Chavez hauled a precarious Amber Scott across the threshold, one hand clamped around her waist as the inebriated woman hung from the Sheriff's shoulder.

"Public intoxication," Chavez grunted as Amber wobbled and lost her balance. "Next time, I'll have to book her."

Liam was unfazed. "This way," he directed, flipping on a light switch that washed the living room in a pale glow. "I'll help you get her into bed." He took up position on the left side of his mother, assisting Chavez as they muscled Amber into a dismal bedroom with bare walls and clothing in every state of cleanliness strewn from the lowboy dresser to the door.

Liam kicked a brown suede boot out of his way, guiding his mom to the unmade bed. "You just sleep this off, Mom."

Amber Scott mumbled something that sounded like, "My boy," and flopped onto the dingy mattress, asleep on contact.

Sheriff Chavez helped Liam get her shoes off, then watched him tuck her in as if it were a practiced skill—which of course it was.

They exited into the living room and Liam shut the bedroom door gently behind them. "Thanks for bringing her home, Sheriff," he said with a quiet but profound sadness.

"Trust me, it would've been easier to take her back to the station and let her sober up in a cell," Chavez replied. "I'm short-handed enough right now."

Liam shifted uncomfortably. "Yeah, we all heard about Deputy Halverson," he frowned, scratching his head. "What happened, exactly?"

Chavez fixed Liam with a parental gaze— one he didn't get from anyone else in his life, especially his own mother. Although she wasn't required to tell this civilian teen anything pertaining to department business, she also saw it as a teaching moment. "Pete apparently got himself into some trouble," she explained. "And that trouble became too much to bear, and he rowed out in his boat and shot himself."

Liam winced, and Chavez noticed.

"You okay?"

"Yeah...yeah," Liam replied almost too quickly. But he wasn't okay. Hearing her say it made the situation real. It was confirmation of a truth so terrible he hated to have to think of it. And it had nothing to do with the story Chavez had just recited. "I'm sorry," he said. "Pete was a stand-up guy, even if we did flip him some shit, occasionally."

Chavez cracked a half smile. "Occasionally?" She ambled toward the door, Liam shuffling beside her. "You fed it to him on a daily basis."

"Yeah, but we did it out of love…"

Liam smiled wistfully, going silent again. Chavez noticed.

"How's your cousin?" she asked, steering the topic onto a side street.

Liam was thankful for the diversion, although there wasn't much to tell her. "Eren? Ah, we haven't heard from her in awhile." A shrug and a sigh followed in short order. He was actually telling God's honest truth. They hadn't heard from Eren since the last summer cookout on the river, almost a year ago.

Chavez saw his expression. "Pity. She was nice. Had a good impact on your little group, and on the town. I hoped you were keeping in touch." She stopped at the front door, giving him a playful nudge. "You're doing good, kiddo. Hold onto those friends of yours. Stay out of trouble."

Liam opened the door for her, his mouth giving the barest hint of a smile.

She turned, nodding toward Amber's bedroom. "And see if you can get her into a program. I have some flyers down at the office."

Liam sighed again, shoulders hunched in resignation. "I'll try, but you and I both know it won't take."

Chavez put a gentle hand on his shoulder. "The point is to try. This won't last forever. One way or another, life will move on."

Liam watched as the sheriff returned to her vehicle, keyed the ignition, and drove away. He finally withdrew back into the house and locked the front door.

Down the wooded street sat an unmarked black Ford sedan. Four dark figures huddled within, listening intently under their studio headphones. The only hint of something out of the ordinary was the tiniest play of moonlight across the parabolic mic dish aimed out the window at the Scott residence.

Track 7:
WASHED UP AND LEFT FOR DEAD

The Selecter (1981)

The Thursday evening dinner rush at the Silver City Diner came to a finish with minimal casualties. The modest restaurant, now cleared of all but a few regulars and stragglers, smelled of the daily special: meat loaf.

It wasn't entirely unpleasant, and A.J. and his friends were hungry.

The gang occupied themselves as they waited for their dinner to arrive and Kris to finish his shift, using their usual booth as a base of operations. In the former coat-check room that now functioned as a limited "arcade", Molly spun the paddle of the new *Tempest* game that Mr. Korolewski brought in to replace the old 1973 Midway *Duck Hunt* monstrosity. Liam padded his high score on the *Asteroids* cabinet next to her.

The jukebox gurgled out "Don't Let Go", the recent single from Wang Chung's *Points on the Curve* album. It was the direct result of Kris and his dad discovering the song on a road trip to Portland over Spring Break.

Chlöe sat in the booth, wound tensely like a spring, thumbing the corner of a wallet photo. She was seriously missing Bodhi, who would not return from his German backpacking trip until mid-July. Gazing wistfully at the picture, she saw Molly's older brother, his tan complexion, hair sun-bleached and feathered, face angled with a sly smile. Having been at college out of state, and now European traveler, he had the mark of a man of the world, and Chlöe felt she could barely contain herself until she saw him again.

A.J. sat opposite her, trying not to stare as she absently played with her straw with her tongue or ran a slender finger up and down its length. He kept sipping the Coke from the red plastic cup and sneaking glances across the restaurant at Lori Tran, sitting alone at her table for two, sketching on an art pad. More than once, she looked up and caught him, and he quickly shifted his gaze at the ceiling, or out the window. Wherever he could look without seeing what Chlöe was doing to that poor straw.

Finally Kris brought the gang's order to the table, and that was enough to draw Molly away from the new wireframe hotness in the game room. Liam followed a few moments later, his quarter having plumbed the depths of his ability to pulverize space rocks on a video screen.

As the teens attacked their plates of food and Kris finished busing the last of the tables, the lively conversation adhered to Bodhi's anticipated arrival, and everyone's plans for the summer. But after several minutes, A.J.'s expression darkened, and he leaned forward with a conspiratorial flair.

"So, um," he began, clearing his throat with a nervous look over his shoulder. "Has anyone...um..."

"Seen your mom naked?" Liam finished his sentence, nodding with faux gravitas. "Yes. Yes, I'm afraid so."

A.J. spit a glob of half-chewed steak fries onto the table, eliciting echoes of disgust from the group.

Chlöe scowled, repulsed. "Oh my *gawd*."

"Dude," Liam chuckled, winking. "Sick."

Molly set her burger down in frustration, gesturing across the table at him. "What. Spit it out, man!"

"And not like you just did," Chlöe added.

"Goddamn it," A.J. fumed. He wasn't sure if he was angrier at Liam for the inappropriate remark, or the fact that he was caught off-guard by behavior that was completely normal for the guy. Or embarrassed at the wet food projectile which had overshot his plate and now lay in the center of the table. "I'm fucking serious here."

Although the group was fueled by snark and banter most of the time, when one of them put on a particular expression, the wagons circled and everyone followed suit.

"Sorry, man," Liam said somewhat contritely. "What's up?"

A.J. took a deep breath, looking at each in turn. "Has anyone used their brands? Like to travel to any of the portals? Maybe to Old Town Calico? Or anywhere else?"

A silent and curious pause descended on the booth. Chlöe finished her bite and gulped down some Coke to chase it.

Molly found A.J.'s eyes. "We agreed we weren't going to do that," she said.

Liam nodded agreement. "That's right."

"I know," A.J. replied. "That's why I'm asking. Has anyone been using the glyphs?"

His question was answered by a confused but collective shaking of heads in the negative.

Molly sucked the last of her root beer through the straw, making the amplified *slurp* noise every parent hated. "Looks like nobody has," she summed up. "Why?"

"Because I saw a phantom last night."

Another silent moment settled over the group as each one let the revelation sink in. Chlöe shivered.

Liam nervously bit his lower lip. "Where?"

"Outside my place. Right after you dropped me off."

Kris arrived at the booth, having shed his apron behind the counter. He pulled a chair to the outside edge of the table. "What happened outside your place?"

"He saw another ghost," Molly answered with quiet reserve.

Kris' eyes grew wide. "Wait. What? They're back? But we haven't seen any in..."

"In over a year," Liam finished.

Chlöe's breath quickened. "Are you kidding me?"

Kris didn't like the sound of this at all. According to Eren, use of a teleportation technology in a local area tended to weaken the fabric of spacetime which kept the various dimensions from overlapping...or something like that.

Liam placed his hands onto the table on either side of his mostly-empty plate. "Hold up. Let's everybody relax and get some more info before we go shitting our pants about this." He turned to A.J. "Was it just the one, or were there a bunch of them, like at the McCabe place?"

"Just the one." A.J. shivered, remembering the seemingly endless parade of specters that had marched from the nexus in the abandoned mansion on the hill above town. Halloween, almost two years ago. The old house was full of them, and they spilled out onto the front yard, and down the road, straight through the middle of town. It was an experience he never wanted to repeat. Especially since they'd shown a tendency to inhabit the bodies of the unconscious.

Molly pressed on. "Did it mess with you at all?"

"No. She looked at me, but then she just floated away and disappeared into the trees at the end of the street."

"And it was a woman," Kris confirmed, trying to lighten the tone. "Not the ghost of Pete Halverson?"

Liam sat back suddenly against the booth, eyes darting nervously around the restaurant interior. It wasn't subtle. Something was eating at him. They all could see it.

A.J. reached across the table, but fell short of contact with Liam's shirt sleeve. "Yo. Dude. What's wrong, man?"

Liam continued scanning the room, expanding his view to the small parking lot outside. He seemed to be looking for something—or someone—in particular.

Kris was scared out of his wits at the strange behavior, and his face had it on full display. Sure, Liam tended toward paranoia, although not nearly as much as A.J. But who wouldn't be, after the year of ghost-fighting, dimension-jumping, and world-saving they'd done?

Following A.J.'s lead, Molly reached out and gently squeezed Liam's hand with her own. "Hey. What is it?"

He leaned forward, his voice a hoarse whisper. "Halverson didn't kill himself."

"Are you shitting me??" Kris uttered breathlessly, suddenly hyper-aware of his volume. A few locals glanced up from their meals at him.

A.J. fought back a wave of creeping dread and swallowed it. He glanced over to where Lori Tran sat sketching, and was briefly overcome with sadness at the prospect of getting involved with someone like her. It seemed like his little group was destined to be caught up in the middle of the weirdest trouble, and bringing someone new into that dynamic wouldn't be fair. Not to her.

He pushed the momentary distraction aside and returned his attention to Liam. "Okay, clearly something's going on here." He locked eyes with Liam and spoke in a hushed tone. "You wanna fill us in, buddy?"

Liam sighed. "Yeah. But not here."

Track 8:
WITNESS

Cyndi Lauper (1983)

Unwilling—or too terrified—to say anything more at the diner, Liam waited until the gang settled into the Reynolds' basement to tell the story he'd been keeping to himself for the past two days.

Everyone filed silently into the rec room. Molly distributed cans of soda from the mini fridge by rote, each person opening their own beverage with the familiar burst of air exploding from the tab.

As his friends found seats among the secondhand furniture in front of the old color television, Liam scooted onto the pool table, dangling a pair of skinny legs over the edge. The stained glass lamp suspended overhead gave him an eerie backlit halo.

Molly and Kris sat together with Chlöe on the sofa, while A.J. flopped down in the recliner with ragged flower-print upholstery which smelled vaguely of stale pipe smoke.

"Hit us, man," A.J. said, his face riddled with concern.

Liam took a breath, then leaned forward, speaking softly as if in a church confessional booth. "Okay, so after we went home on Tuesday night, I went out to our hangout on the spit by the river, to smoke a joint and watch the meteor shower."

Molly raised a fist of approved. "My man."

"I wanted to be alone for awhile," Liam continued, "to get my head right. Shit's not great at home right now. Mom's drinking again, and it's getting worse."

A.J. sighed. "That sucks, dude."

"Yeah, it does," Liam said, more than a bit snippy in his reply. He knew A.J. meant well, but he still bristled at the interruption. "So anyway, I'm out there, lying back on the sandbar, and I see a little boat drifting down from up-river. Two people in it. One of 'em looks like Halverson, you know, just from his build. He's hard to miss. And it's his boat—I've seen him in that thing so many times. His place is up-river from that spot. So I figure he's out trying to clear his head too, maybe have a brewski with a buddy."

A.J. frowned. "Halverson doesn't have any 'buddies'."

"Yeah," Kris added. "That's sketchy as hell."

"You're sure it was him?" Molly pressed.

"A hundred percent. He was wearing his cop jacket and his hat. I could even make out most of his face in the moonlight."

"But you didn't recognize the other person?"

Liam shook his head no.

A.J. squinted. "And he was just out for a little moonlight cruise in his aluminum fishing dinghy..."

Liam sighed. "Yeah, dude. You know how many times I've seen him on the river late at night when I've been out there too?"

"Seventeen times?" Kris offered. His comment was met with a collective stare of exasperation from the group.

"So anyway, it wasn't too unusual for Halverson to be out there, but I've never seen him with anyone else—not at night on the river. And the other weird thing was that this other dude was pretty busy, moving around like he was working on something. And Halverson just kinda sat completely still."

"Super weird," Chlöe mused, to much nodded agreement.

Liam shifted his weight on the pool table and nervously cleared his throat. "So at one point, the second person in the boat stood up in front of Halverson, and I heard a muffled gunshot—like with a suppressor—and Halverson's brains just exploded out the back of his skull."

He could feel the disgust from that last detail radiating back at him.

Molly scrunched her nose. "Ugh. Nasty."

"Anyway, the mystery man just slipped into the water and disappeared. Halverson slumped over sideways, and eventually he went into the river too." Liam finally looked up and scanned around the room to find every occupant staring at him in shock.

"Are you shitting me?" A.J. gasped, recalling Kris' exclamation in the diner.

"Wish I was," Liam replied, eyes downcast. "I just froze. Held completely still until the boat had drifted well past me down-river. Saw some motion on the far bank as the mystery guy got out and disappeared into the forest. At that point I booked it home." He paused, finding his thoughts and putting them in order. "Halverson didn't kill himself like Chavez told me. And honestly, I think he was dead by the time he was in the boat. Someone shot his corpse—probably with his own sidearm—to make it look like suicide."

The group shuddered as one organism. Chlöe clasped her arms around her knees and hugged them close.

"The cops did find his gun, and it'd apparently been fired," Molly said. "But I didn't hear anything about a silencer."

"Mystery guy probably took it with him." Liam folded his arms and cast his gaze back to the rust colored carpet. "I don't think that supposed 'scandal' was anything either."

Chlöe squinted. "Okay, but how do you know for sure?"

A.J. frowned. "We never saw any evidence of impropriety or hanging out with underage girls."

"Pete Halverson had the nickname Ranger Rick for a reason," Liam said. "He could be a colossal douchebag, but he was as squeaky clean as they make 'em."

Kris repeatedly kicked his foot in nervous apprehension. "We have to tell Chavez," he said in earnest. "We have to tell the sheriff."

"Hold up there, cowboy." Molly stood, pacing the floor next to the coffee table. "We don't know who actually killed him, or why."

"Yeah," A.J. agreed. "Or why they tried to set him up with that scandal in the first place."

"That time the car tried to run us off the bridge," Kris recalled, "and the Project Black Eagle agents? They're federal level, guys. We can't just sit on this."

A.J. rubbed his eyes. The Project Black Eagle Kris referred to was the gang's nickname for the seemingly endless supply of mysterious federal agents who had menaced them during the Summer of '82. The name was derived from the stylized eagle image printed on some of their vehicles, and on signs within their hidden laboratory facility in the forest. It was, oddly—or perhaps appropriately—the same image sported on the flight suit patch worn by the Black Eagle Squadron, a unit of soldiers from a parallel Earth. "Exactly," he sighed. "They're feds. There won't be anything Chavez or the Curry Country Sheriff's Department can do to protect us if they find out."

"They're not just feds," Liam corrected. His throat was hoarse and dry. "They're black ops, man. They murdered a goddamn sheriff's deputy. They can do the same to us. They made Eren's friends on the recovery team disappear. They can make us disappear too."

A.J. locked eyes with Kris. "We have to be a hundred percent united on this. Let it lie. We hold our cards for the time being."

"And nobody says anything to anybody without a pow wow beforehand," Molly insisted.

Liam nodded thoughtfully. "Fuckin' ay."

"At least for a few days," A.J. added. "Just to see how this all shakes out."

The parties agreed, and each put a hand out in a team gesture. Liam was the last to add his hand to the pile, looking at each friend in turn. "Not a damn word," he instructed.

◌℞

Butch Carlton negotiated the curve on Jerry's Flat Road across the river from the pulp mill. The frontage took his rusted Chevy pickup nearer to the riverbank before diverging again on its way to Gold Beach.

His cooler was packed with freshly-caught steelhead trout and an impressive Coho salmon procured at a spot just east of the Myrtletree Bridge. A recent retiree from the Forest Service, Carlton knew all the best fishing spots in the area, and couldn't wait to get the salmon in his smoker. The steelhead would be dinner.

With the warm lights of Calico piercing the night from the north bank, Butch traversed the northernmost arm of Coyote Riffle, a tributary of the Rogue. The second arm followed, and he could see the industrial lights of the salmon cannery overlooking Canfield Bar as he approached another 90-degree curve.

He knew every inch of state route 595 by feel, could anticipate every dip and turn from memory. He was aware of the unnamed logging spur leading from the impending curve into the deep woods. But he was not anticipating the rhythmic flash of hazard lights from a disabled vehicle, nosed into the trees.

As he reduced speed and drew closer to the flashing hazards, he determined the car to be a mid-'70s Dodge station wagon. The factory paint job—either eggshell or parchment, he couldn't be sure in the stark headlights—was scuffed and pocked with rust. A darker-colored panel ran around the outside.

Butch suddenly realized that he knew both the car and its owner, Mary Grisham. She operated a small grocery in Gold Beach, and was not known as a person who probed the logging trails of Curry County after dark in her station wagon. The hood wasn't raised, but the hazards were going, and the passenger door was open, keeping the interior dome light from shutting off. That eliminated a dead battery, but something was definitely wrong.

He slowed, pulling onto the shoulder just short of the spur, shifting into PARK and leaving the engine running. He reached across to punch open the glove box, and withdrew a plastic flashlight.

A light blanket of late spring mist hugged the ground as Butch stepped from the truck and flicked the flashlight on. The beam was redundant, given that the headlamps on the truck fully illuminated the station wagon, which, Butch now saw was cocked at an angle on the dirt road, blocking the spur almost totally.

"Mary?" he hailed, to no reply.

The station wagon's headlights cast their own beam into the woods to the south side of the logging trail, and Butch could make out a subtle motion near the front of the car. It created an eerie shadow play on the veil of mist below the evergreens, and Butch squinted into the distance.

"Hey, Mary! You alright over there?" Perhaps she was struggling with the jack to fix a flat tire.

He tread closer to the wagon, aiming the flashlight through its large rear windows, unable to see anything out of place—until he came around the front fender. The driver's seat and headrest were painted crimson with blood and viscera.

Butch froze in place, his breath caught in his throat. The flashlight beam tracked down across the hood of the car, coming to rest on a scene so horrible that his brain refused to comprehend it.

Fifty-year-old Mary Grisham sat propped against the front grille, silver-blond hair matted with sweat. She was slender, and clothed only in the blood of a second figure clasped between her limbs much as a spider would hold its paralyzed prey. The victim was also female, and lay limp in Mary's embrace, any spark of life long gone. Most of the corpse's right shoulder and neck were missing—gnawed away—and dead eyes stared into the night.

It was in that moment that Butch Carlton made an impossible realization: the corpse was *also* Mary Grisham.

To him it appeared that Mary was in the process of devouring her own dead body. Or that of an identical twin. But how could that be? It was too bizarre, too unthinkable. True, Curry County had its share of weird happenings, but cannibal doppelgangers weren't usually on the bill.

"Dear God..." Butch whispered to no one in particular, but it got Mary's attention.

Her gaze darted upward at him, face and chin smeared dark red. Her teeth bared in a bizarre grin, glistening bloody in the flashlight's beam. A sound unlike any he'd ever heard—human or animal—rumbled from deep within her ribcage.

The feeling returned to his legs as the *flight* part of his fight-or-flight instinct kicked in. He turned to run back to the safety of his truck, to get the hell out of there, but an enormous shadow blocked his way.

He glanced up to see multiple glossy garnet-red eyes reflecting in the dark, and then something pierced the side of his neck and he felt his body go numb. The world turned sideways, and he was vaguely aware of falling to the ground, able to see the wheels of his pickup truck and hear the thrum of its idling engine. Then something rolled him onto his back, and he found himself looking up at his own face, his own body, pale and naked in the headlights.

But it *wasn't* him, was it? It *couldn't* be.

His view shifted again as the mirror image above him lowered close, turning his head to the side. He felt pressure in the crook of his neck, then the sensation of slipping into a dream.

The lights of Calico shimmered across the Rogue, and slowly went dim.

Track 9:
IN THE DARK
Romeo Void (1982)

The black sedan started following them a block from Molly's.

Liam noticed almost immediately, and A.J. didn't need to ask when he saw his friend repeatedly glance at the reflected headlights in the rear view mirror. Despite Liam's tactic of weaving a leisurely, meandering course through town, the car kept with them—far enough back to make them second guess themselves for the first half-dozen turns.

A.J. squinted through his glasses at the lights behind them. "Dude, is that...?"

"You know it is," Liam deadpanned. "Fuckers."

At Pioneer and 3rd, Liam swerved into the Value-Drug parking lot and killed his headlights. There were still a few vehicles sitting there, awaiting their drivers' return.

They sat for several seconds, blood pulsing in their ears, waiting for the mysterious car to pass the drugstore, but it never did. A.J. began to fidget.

"Dude, let's split up," he suggested, waving a thumb at his bike in the bed of the El Camino. "I'll ride home, you keep snaking your way and make sure it's what we think it is."

Liam nodded in agreement. "Keep out of the light as much as you can."

"I will," A.J. promised. "And you be careful. Call me when you get home so I know you made it okay. If you get in any trouble go straight to the sheriff."

"As much as it pains me to agree with that part of the plan," Liam muttered, "I think you're right."

The two boys clasped hands with each other as they parted, A.J. hauling his bike from the back of the vehicle and retreating with it to a shadow near the front window of the drugstore.

As he watched, Liam started the El Camino and casually rolled out of the parking lot, heading east on Third Avenue. An old yellow VW Beetle sputtered along behind him. A.J almost relaxed, but then he saw the black sedan pick up the trail, following down the block past the office center at Cedar Street.

A.J. swung his leg across the seat of his bike and pushed it forward, stepping onto the pedals as they rotated. Keeping the tail lights of the sedan in view, he took the same route along 3rd, following the follower. He should have been terrified, but adrenaline being such a powerful drug, he found he actually felt more like James Bond than a teenager avoiding federal surveillance.

Liam suddenly took a hard right at Cantor Street, heading south to the riverfront with the sedan on its trail, while the Beetle continued straight. A.J. continued through the intersection, casting a quick look to his right for a glimpse of those red tail lights. Liam was on his own now, at least for the duration of the drive home.

A.J. sped along 3rd through the center of town, passing businesses now closed for the night. He took a left on Main Street, across the green space between 3rd and Pioneer, then a right on 4th, standing in the saddle to pump the pedals up the hill as he finally turned onto Lamont Street. There was little car traffic here, but A.J. continued to check back over his shoulder every few seconds, just to be sure he wasn't being followed.

The home stretch was a zig-zag route through the residential area on the lower hill above Calico proper. Ash Street didn't have the views that Cantor Heights, Cedar Heights, or Timber Hill Road did. But it was a step up from the double-wides and manufactured homes where Liam lived, east of the Junior High.

He cruised up to the modest craftsman home at the end of the block, standing on the left pedal as he dismounted in one graceful motion. He propped the bike against the back column of the carport, near the front of his dad's silver Buick Skylark. Clearing the lower three steps to the landing by the back door, A.J. blew in like a cyclone.

"Hey Mom, hey Dad," he greeted with a brief wave before disappearing into his room.

His parents were cuddled on the sofa in front of the new episode of *Magnum P.I.* "Hey sport," his dad said, managing to get the first word out before A.J.'s bedroom door slammed shut. "How was your...day?"

His parents shrugged to one another, resigned to their current reality. They knew things could be far worse. A.J. did well in school. He had a summer job. He had friends to be social with.

At least he wasn't in trouble with the law.

A.J. paced back and forth between the foot of his bed and the desk in the corner, where he did most of his writing. Vast fantasy worlds and complex, layered adventures had been conceived here. But this was unfortunately no fantasy tale he was living. Some mysterious government agency was tracking him—or at the very least his close friend—and had already assassinated a sheriff's deputy. This was the kind of tangled web of conspiracy he'd indulged in since childhood, and now he was finding it far too real for his liking.

If things went well, it should only be a few more minutes until Liam arrived home. Until then, A.J. figured the best thing to do was try to relax. Writing usually calmed his nerves, but he dared not jot down anything that might become evidence at some point. And he was too wired and unfocused to work on his fantasy story.

He just needed to take a few deep breaths, and wait for Liam's phone call. If he got home without further interference from the black sedan, maybe it was just routine surveillance and things weren't quite as dire as A.J. assumed.

Oh, who was he kidding?

It was always dire.

A.J. flopped down in the office swivel chair in front of his desk, pulling out his *Dungeon Master's Guide* hardcover from the stack of roleplaying manuals. He took in the cover painting of various fantasy adventurers locked in combat with a giant red *efrit*—a demon from Persian tradition.

A sudden, blinding flash saturated A.J.'s view, momentarily whiting out the book cover illustration, and he could hear the contained *whoosh* of air displaced. Papers ruffled and shifted on his desk.

The shiver along his spine spread up into his scalp, and his face flushed. He knew before he turned around that someone had used a teleport glyph to "jump" into his bedroom. But he didn't dare hope that it was who he wanted it to be.

"Hello, A.J."

The voice was low and soft, feminine with a weary edge.

A.J. turned in the chair. Sitting cross-legged on his bed was a young woman with a slim, athletic frame. Her skin was tan and smooth, shoulder-length raven hair sporting a green tint that matched her eyes. As she rose from the bed to her feet, A.J. noticed she was wearing the same outfit he'd last seen her in: black jeans tucked into short Doc Marten boots, and a black motorcycle jacket over a Killing Joke concert tee.

"Eren," he whispered in disbelief.

She offered a tentative smile. "Do I get a hug, or..."

Before he knew it, A.J. was on his feet, swept into her embrace. "Whoa," she marveled. "You've gotten taller." She stepped back, looking him over and giving his shoulders a squeeze. "And buff, too."

A.J. chuckled. "Had a growth spurt. This is nothing. Wait 'til you see Kris. Dude's a total stud now."

"That doesn't surprise me," Eren laughed.

A.J. suddenly remembered his parents in the living room, and signaled Eren that they'd have to keep their voices down. Gesturing for her to have a seat on the bed, he turned on the boombox which sat in the corner of his desk, continuing one of Molly's recent mix tapes in mid-song.

Pale Shelter by Tears For Fears erupted from the speakers, and A.J. adjusted the volume loud enough to cover their voices but low enough so as not to disrupt his parents' television viewing.

"You look good, A.J." Eren said, sitting on the edge of the twin bed as he pulled the desk chair closer. "I can't wait to see the gang."

"They'll be so happy to see you," A.J. replied.

They stared at each other for several seconds, time which for any other two people would have seemed awkward. But for A.J., being in Eren's presence had a calming effect no drug could duplicate. He didn't particularly care if they never spoke another word. But gradually her expression shifted from joy at their reunion to the sad and worried look he'd only seen the day before she left, and it brought him back to reality.

"Okay," he sighed. "What are you doing here?"

Track 10:

HUNTER AND THE HUNTED

Simple Minds (1982)

Liam decided to test the abilities of his tail, taking a hard right at the end of the block between the post office and the gas station. By the next left, all pretext of a sane route home was out the window. The El Camino's engine growled as he sped south on Evelyn Street, toward 1st Avenue, hitting another sharp right at the Electro-Shack.

The Sand Bar lounge was hopping for a Thursday night, gravel parking lot full of questionable rides home come closing time. Tires shrieked as Liam fishtailed in another hard turn south on Cedar Street, heading toward the riverfront warehouses. He flew past Mama's Deli and the fish & chips joint on his right, before spying the red neon of Leo's Tavern, his mom's place of business. Another collection of vehicles sat parked in a cratered asphalt lot with no painted spaces or curbs.

For an instant, Liam considered pulling into the tavern lot and hiding within the sad bunch of cars until the tail gave up, but then he caught the flash of headlights following him onto Cedar, and thought it best to press on as quickly as possible.

His car caught air as it crested the top of the hill at Leo's, and Liam momentarily fancied himself Steve McQueen in the classic car chase from *Bullitt*. Then he was blazing down lower Cedar past the warehouses and a ninety-degree turn onto North Bank Rogue River Road. The roadside barrier along the frontage was minimal—just a thin galvanized strip at knee height running about twenty feet across the T intersection before disappearing. He'd have to be precise here. If his steering or speed was off as he drifted into the turn, he could flip the vehicle, or skid off the road. Either option meant most likely ending up in the river itself.

Fortunately this wasn't his first time driving this route at speed, and he nailed the turn with a slight fishtail as his rear tires desperately screamed for traction on the pavement. North Bank Road was infamously squirrelly, pitted from weather, logging traffic, and the occasional flooding when the Rogue crested its banks. Driving the stretch between the back of the warehouses and the pulp mill was a game of "pothole slalom", and Liam had the local high score.

Gripping the steering wheel, he zipped left and right between the gaps and buckled berms. He approached the corner of the mill before he saw the sedan's headlights turning onto the frontage from the bottom of the hill, and he thought he might have a chance to shake them if he could maintain the lead.

Glancing down at the speedometer, he saw he was doing just over 60 miles per hour, in a zone marked 40. If he passed a sheriff's deputy vehicle, it would all be over, but then he wouldn't have to worry about the sedan, or the people in it.

He was coming up on the Y intersection where 1st Avenue merged with the frontage road, jogging east and north around the Junior High School before following the river toward Old Town Calico. Much like the Sand Bar and Leo's, the Calico Saloon was packed with locals sharing one more round before closing for the night. As far as he could tell, the stop at the end of 1st Avenue was devoid of traffic. Taking a deep breath, Liam offered up a vague prayer to his indigenous ancestors to make sure his path remained clear.

Just as he finished his silent plea to the fates, an old Dodge pickup paused at the stop sign and began to roll through onto the frontage. Liam cursed under his breath and stepped on his brakes, coming up behind the Dodge's rusted bed as it trundled up the road past the saloon. Glancing up at the rear view mirror, Liam saw distant headlights draw closer. There was half a block to cover until the rusted Dodge would either make a left on Silver Street or continue on North Bank Rogue River Road. He planned to take whichever option the old pickup didn't.

The lights in this mirror brightened, and Liam could tell the sedan was closing the gap between them. He didn't have much time. Miraculously, the driver of the pickup hit his left turn signal, and as the vehicle parted to turn up Silver Street, Liam gunned his accelerator and hit the 45-degree curve by the Junior High, tires squealing.

This stretch of frontage along the south side of the school was in relatively good repair, and Liam took the opportunity to build up speed. Because of the change in angle, he could no longer track his pursuer. He hoped they were trapped behind a line of rusty Dodge pickups rolling through the stop at 1st Avenue, but knew that wasn't the most likely of scenarios.

The road took a sharp curve northeast, following the bend in the river. It was a long straightaway heading out of downtown Calico and into the rural neighborhoods, like Ever-green Drive, where Liam lived, and the trailer park on Lakeshore. As he sped up the road along the east side of the school, his mirror gleamed once again, and he knew his tail was back on him.

The last thing he wanted to do was to lead them directly back to his home. It was time to get creative.

At the end of the straightaway, the frontage contorted into another 90-degree bend. But a rural lane called River Drive extended north along the shore of a small lake which was a tributary of the Rogue. River Drive crept up the hill, back into the woods—woods that sheltered a myriad of old logging spurs and teen hideaways.

If he took the right turn and kept on the North Bank road, he could be home in about four minutes. The lights grew larger and brighter in the rear view mirror.

It was decision time.

Liam felt the El Camino shoot left onto Riv-er Drive, engine roaring up the hill. There were no streetlights, and scarcely any homes. The odd trailer set back from the road, breaking up the flat black expanse of the forest with a tiny square of light. By and large, the only real illumination came from Liam's car and the sedan following him.

He'd led the tail on quite the meandering chase through town, and the fact that they were still on his ass told him they were not playing around. And that worried him.

The chassis of the El Camino jostled and thumped as the pavement gave way to gravel, and the potholes got deeper and wider in diameter. A short distance ahead, River Drive split onto one of the many logging trails used when the town's major export was timber. He knew the spur ran across the hill, and was thick with pines. The trail was one he knew well—his crew had grown up exploring the area on their bikes, often riding at night, with only a pale moon lighting their way.

As the El Camino rumbled across the ancient truck bridge onto the logging trail, Liam cut his lights. It was suddenly very dark, and a lot more dangerous. The dirt road wandered through sparse woods, gradually becoming thicker with trees.

Liam checked his mirrors. The sedan's headlights were distant, but they were still on his trail.

A burned out redwood sat in a grove just off the road, and Liam recalled it to be an ideal hiding place. But if he pulled in and stopped, especially within the "safety" of the massive tree stump, he was counting on his pursuers to overlook him, limiting his options. No, he would continue on the logging trail, running dark, hoping the agents in the black sedan would get lost in the labyrinth of dirt roads and deer paths on the hill above Calico.

After another five minutes of zig-zagging dirt trails in the dark, Liam could no longer see the sedan's headlights in his mirrors.

Eventually the trail met with the end of Papoose Drive, which ran at a northwest-southeast diagonal and connected with the frontage road at the bottom of the hill. It also happened to intersect with West Evergreen about a block away from Liam's house. Although not the quality of the neighborhoods closer to downtown, Papoose was paved at the very least, and Liam continued on his homeward trajectory with his headlights off.

He pulled into the driveway, noting a certain brown and white Bronco belonging to Sheriff Chavez on the street in front of his house. She appeared to be doing some paperwork or reading through a file by the cab light, but saw Liam arrive and got out to greet him.

"Something wrong with your headlights?" she asked as Liam stood from the driver's seat and slammed the door.

He shrugged. "Fuse, I think."

She knew he was lying, but didn't push it beyond a warning. "Shouldn't be driving at night without your lights, amigo."

"Yeah, I know." He leaned against the car door, folding his arms. "You didn't come out here to give me a safety lesson, did you?"

Chavez stood by the front grill of the Bronco, resting a work boot against the winch assembly. "I came to tell you your mom's in custody."

Liam took a breath and rolled his eyes, bracing for the rest. "What is it this time?"

"What is it every time? Public intoxication. She's sleeping it off tonight." Chavez removed her foot from the bumper and slowly approached Liam in the driveway. "You okay, *mijo?*"

Liam shifted nervously, eyes probing down the street. "I uh...I'm okay. Just mom...and stuff." He knew immediately that she wasn't convinced, so he angled the topic away. "Hey, what do you think of the whole Halverson deal? Seems kinda sketchy to me."

"Really?" Chavez squinted, hands on hips. "You know something you wanna tell me?"

Liam shrugged. "Just curious, I guess. He didn't seem the type to want to kill himself. Or do any of the stuff he was rumored to."

The sheriff took a breath, her expression softening for a moment. "Look. I didn't tell you this, but I received a file with alleged 'evidence' of Pete being caught up with underage girls, giving them alcohol, and transporting them across state lines," she said, adding in air-quotes, "for immoral purposes."

"You don't believe that."

"No, I don't believe that. Of course not. Not for an instant." Chavez looked at her hand, scratching at a hangnail with her thumb. "But it was from a federal source, so I can't just dismiss it."

"You think he was set up?"

"I know he was set up. Pete was looking into the crashed device in the forest and why it disappeared shortly after the feds arrived on the scene."

Liam shoved his hands into his front pockets and shrugged again. "Maybe he was getting close to something."

Chavez nodded, lost in thought. Blinking suddenly, she snapped back to reality and waved a finger at Liam as she returned to the Bronco. "Regardless, you and your buddies keep clear of this, eh? I'm doing you a courtesy because you know about the crash site and I don't want you thinking I'm not working on this. And I never discussed the matter with you." She pulled open the driver's side door and peered over it. "I'll release your mom tomorrow. You be okay on your own tonight?"

"Yeah," Liam offered a halfhearted salute, heading toward the house, pausing at the door to watch the Bronco drive away.

You be okay on your own tonight? rang in his head. What a stupid question. They both knew he was on his own *every* night.

Track 11:
THE REFUGEE
U2 (1983)

"Well now we know why the phantoms are back," A.J. mused, turning toward his desk as the mix tape clicked to a stop. His boombox wasn't one of those fancy-shmancy ones with auto-reverse; you actually had to pop the tape out and flip it over to continue. He pressed *PLAY*, plopping onto the rolling desk chair again and sliding it back over by the bed. The curated playlist of British alternative music growled and pulsed from the speakers.

"Yeah, sorry," Eren sighed. "Not much we can do about that. I hope they're not causing any problems."

A.J. recalled the shimmering phantom woman from the other night, wafting past him down the street. "Not so far," he said. "Although...people gotta sleep."

"It's really good to see you, A.J." Eren smiled.

A.J. tried to play it cool, but couldn't help blushing. "You said that already," he chuckled softly. "And you look amazing, of course. Love your hair like that."

"Oh, hell," she cringed, running slender fingers through the ratty tangle of dark hair with the green tint. "It's a mess. Honestly, I've been too busy to do anything with it, with everything going on."

"Oh yeah?" A.J. was intrigued. This wasn't just a visit then. But of course it wasn't. The resources necessary to travel across dimensions from a parallel Earth were considerable. You didn't just pop over for a casual hello. "What *is* going on?"

"I'm sorry to just show up here on business, but...I'm here on business."

"Shocking," A.J. marveled. "And I thought you just couldn't stay away from all *this*..." He waved a hand down the length of his torso like a game show hostess showing off a brand new car.

Eren bit her lower lip. "Don't sell yourself short, mister. You're filling out in all the right ways." They shared a quiet and perhaps slightly wistful laugh, and Eren averted her gaze to keep her train of thought securely on the tracks. "But I'm here on a mission, and I may need some help."

"Ooh," A.J. blinked, thoughtfully stroking an invisible beard. "Top secret mission from alternate Earth. Gotta activate the local assets."

"*Local assets*," Eren repeated with a throaty chuckle. "You know you guys are more than just *local assets*. You're heroes back home. We owe everything to you."

A.J. nodded, wiggling his fingers. "*Yeah* you do. Without our elite Atari-trained hand-eye coordination, you would have never repelled your space invaders. Alternate Earth would have fallen."

"Um, dude, where I'm from, *this* is 'alternate Earth'. And it's not quite that simple, but yeah. You guys made it possible. So that's why I'm hoping this can be a quick and easy deal."

A.J. cocked his head and leaned back in the desk chair. "That's me. Quick and easy."

"That's not what I told my command back home," Eren smirked.

It had never occurred to A.J that Eren would have told people in her dimension about her friends in this one. "Wait. What? What did you tell them?"

"Oh man," Eren sighed, delighting in the adolescent confusion she'd created in this moment. "You're a legendary stud on my Earth." She paused momentarily, then reiterated: "Legendary."

A.J. swallowed, but his mouth felt like a sandbox. "I guess I need to date in your dimension then."

"Aww, no takers in Calico?" Eren's demeanor suddenly became soft and empathetic, a warmth filling her green eyes with concern.

"Well..." A.J. shrugged, recalling his interaction with Lori Tran at the photo counter. "There is one girl..."

"Ooh, tell me everything." Eren shifted, leaning forward on the edge of the bed.

"Lori," he began. "She's really cool. Photographer...artist. Likes the same music. Really cute."

Eren stared at him, hanging on every word. "She's super into you, I'll bet."

A.J. flushed, blinking back to reality. "What? No, I don't know."

"How could she not be?"

A.J. regarded his guest with an expression between amusement and disbelief. "How do you do that?"

"Do what?"

"How do you just appear and immediately make people feel on top of the world?"

Eren smiled sweetly at him. "I call 'em like I see 'em. That's your baseball saying, right?"

A.J. blushed. "You just have this effortless ability to build people up. Honestly, I could ride this high for a week."

They stared at each other and A.J. couldn't tell if she was truly unaware of her natural charisma, or if she knew and just wasn't letting on.

"It's really disconcerting, y'know."

Eren leaned back, breaking eye contact. "Well, hopefully I won't be in your hair for long."

A.J. took a breath, suddenly released from what felt like a magic spell. "So why *are* you here? What's the mission? And incidentally, why didn't you blink back to Liam's place? You left a glyph in his back yard."

Reeling, Eren held up a hand in protest. "Whoa, okay. One at a time. First off, remember when I turned up here last year, I was following the Black Eagle recovery team who stashed the weapon we used against the Invaders. Command back home presumed the team was either killed or disappeared into the bowels of your federal government."

A.J. nodded, recalling their break-in at the top secret site in the Siskyou Forest, their retrieval of the spacecraft and daring escape from government agents, soldiers and scientists.

"When I went back to the site just before I left, it'd been mothballed, which seemed to confirm that assumption." Eren's expression tightened, and A.J. knew what was coming next.

"We received a message," she said quietly. "They're alive."

A.J. heard a gasp of surprise and realized it had come from his own mouth. "No shit?"

"Well, three of them are. They apparently survived interrogation and escaped custody. They managed to get a message back requesting extraction."

"So you're here to get them out."

"Yeah," Eren nodded. "I'm the taxi service. Or the getaway driver."

A.J. leaned forward with sudden interest. "Do we know where they are?"

"Do *we* know? Well, *we* don't know much, but we think they're holed up somewhere in the area between Hanging Rock and the greater Siskyou Forest."

"That doesn't exactly narrow it down."

"No kidding. It's kind of a big undertaking. I had to decide whether to look for these two needles in a massive haystack myself, or enlist my *local assets.*" Eren made air quotes with her fingers, which caused A.J. to smile. It was something she'd picked up during her previous stay in Calico. "I *really* don't want to have to ask for help again, especially after everything you've already done. But you guys already know my situation, so you don't need an in-depth briefing, and nobody new has to be brought into it. You already have teleport brands, and you know how to jump. I've got a ship stashed up on the mountain, out near Hanging Rock. We can use it to make the rescue and get the hell out of Dodge, hopefully before those feds realize I've been here."

A.J. suddenly flashed a worried look, and Eren's eyes went wide with concern.

"What—?"

"I think the feds may already be onto you," he explained. "We've had another black sedan following us since Deputy Halverson was killed."

It was Eren's turn to gasp. "Pete Halverson died?"

"Yeah. They made it look like a suicide. It's a whole story, but Liam is the best one to catch you up on that."

Still leaning forward, Eren reached out and clasped A.J.'s hands in her own. "That's not good, A.J. I don't want to make more trouble for you guys." She searched his eyes and connected once again. "Look, it's totally cool to say no. I'll deal with the extraction myself and won't bother any of you again."

Although surprised by the overtly tender gesture, he sat still, allowing her hands to warm his. "That's not really the issue," he said. "I'm in, Eren. You know I'm in. But I can't speak for the others. You'll need to talk to them, and get the lowdown on the fed situation from Liam. I think we need a clean slate and full disclosure to move forward." He maneuvered his right hand to grasp hers in the kind of handshake that resembled the start of an arm wrestling contest. "Deal?"

Eren squeezed, feeling their old bond return. "Deal."

"But first," A.J. leaned in close, touching his forehead to hers, "blink your ass to Liam's house, so my parents don't wonder who I'm talking to in here." Pulling away, he had a sudden thought, and went to grab one of the spiral notebooks from his pack. "And if you get a chance, give this a read, see what you think."

"Copy that," Eren said, taking the pad with a smile. She reached into her left sleeve to touch the inside of her wrist, and there was an explosion of light, followed by the shift of local air pressure filling the sudden void.

A.J. inhaled deeply, smelling the ionized atmosphere in his bedroom. He could hear the phone ring in the living room, and the muffled sound of his mom answering. Liam must have arrived home safely, and he was about to get a doozy of a surprise.

☙

Sheriff Chavez paused at the entry door to the riverfront cabin and took a breath. She'd been a visitor at Pete Halverson's place when he was alive, but this was a wholly unique scenario. She hadn't planned on stopping by tonight—Pete's death was still fresh, and she somehow felt it disrespectful to go snooping through his home. Come to think of it, she didn't even know what she hoped to find here, but there was something distinctly *not right* about the whole thing.

For starters, Pete Halverson was far from suicidal. No matter how bad things got, he was one of those annoying optimists who just kept pressing on until a given situation improved. And it usually did. Either that, or he was too dense to gauge the true scale of a bad situation. And this situation had grown far beyond merely "bad". After almost ten years with the Department, with a sterling service record, to find himself under federal investigation...

As the Sheriff of Curry County, Chavez was used to the smell of fish. And this whole deal was fishy on a *completely different level of fishy.*

She tested the handle and it turned, door swinging open into the dark. It wasn't uncommon for folks to leave their front doors unlocked in this rural community, but for someone as security-minded as Pete, it struck her as odd. Reaching inside the entry, she flicked on the light switch. The dwelling was a study in 1970s earth tones and dark wood paneling. And it was clear someone had tossed the place. Not trashed, but searched.

Nothing was broken, but there were enough things out of place that Chavez could tell there had been recent foot traffic, and whoever it was had been looking for something specific, not found it, and left in a hurry. All of the kitchen cupboards were open, and Halverson's stack of *Curry County Reporter* newspapers next to the fireplace was toppled over.

She passed the old mid-century kitchen table which was empty save for a half-empty cup of coffee, long cold. Stepping quietly to the sliding glass door that looked out over the river, Chavez marveled at the majestic view from such a humble cabin. A small boat dock extended into the water from the edge of the modest yard, and she noted his aluminum fishing boat was gone—impounded in departmental custody as evidence, despite an official coroner's report that ruled out foul play. The door shuddered open with an unwilling squeak, and Chavez strode into the small, rocky frontage, illuminated by an exterior spotlight near the door and the reflected moonlight on the water.

She took a deep breath of night air off the river, and was about to turn to leave when she spied a long-necked plastic lighter in the gravel beneath Halverson's outdoor grill. On a whim, she opened the barbecue's rusty cover. It too let out a reluctant groan as she lifted the handle, revealing a single manila folder—crammed absolutely full.

An electric chill shot down her spine as Chavez quickly rifled through the folder's contents: handwritten notes detailing trips to the crash site in the woods from 1982 to 1983, photographs of the location—including the crashed device itself before the feds took it away. And a single snapshot of the painted seal on a black government SUV. It featured no lettering at all, just a stylized black eagle in a white circle. The same logo also showed up on an embroidered patch on A.J.'s denim vest in a photo of the boy and his crew at a summer cookout. There were research notes on something called Project Black Eagle, and a few other photos of various locations around Siskiyou National Forest.

She slapped the folder shut and quickly made her way back to the house, turning off the lights as she left through the front door. This would take some time to comb through, and she sure as hell wasn't going to do it in Halverson's back yard at night, especially if the house was under any kind of federal surveillance. What's more, the fact that Pete had stashed the folder in a barbecue told her that he was afraid of his home being searched, and would make it easier to dispose of if needed. And that meant he knew the feds were onto him.

But of course he did. They were accusing him of an array of illicit acts to make him cease his investigation. That was certainly how it appeared, anyway.

As she drove away, Sheriff Chavez felt every warning signal in the law enforcement compartment of her brain go off at once. None of this was normal, and all of it was highly suspect. Halverson had been a local sheriff's deputy just doing his job, and had been executed—by agents of his own government—for it.

Seconds later, the radio call came through: a Chevy pickup and Dodge station wagon were found abandoned at the logging spur off Route 595, just west of Coyote Riffle. Blood in one of the vehicles. K-9 unit dispatched.

"*¿Qué chingados?*" she muttered, and headed to the scene, Bronco light bar ablaze in red and blue.

Track 12:
ACCENT ON YOUTH
Ultravox (1981)

A.J. wasn't wrong about the "doozy of a surprise".

Having delivered the message of safe arrival to A.J.'s mother, Liam hung up the phone and went to his room to relax before crashing for the night. When he saw the flash of light from his back yard, he nearly spilled the contents of the plastic baggy in his lap, along with most of his rolling papers.

Eren had chosen a good night to arrive, what with Amber Scott enjoying the hospitality of the Curry County Jail. She came to the back door, assuming the front was under surveillance, and Liam immediately wrapped her in a tight hug.

"Howdy, stranger," he grunted, breath squeezed from his lungs with Eren's embrace.

"Hey there, 'cousin'."

Liam paused suddenly, as the various puzzle pieces began to assemble in his mind. "You're not here for a visit."

Eren offered a wistful smile, catlike eyes piercing the dim light of the manufactured home. "A.J. says you're having some trouble with the feds?" she deflected.

"You have no idea," Liam sighed. "And don't change the subject."

Eren grinned more heartily at the comment. "Well, don't just stand there. Gimme a Coke and let's catch up."

Liam led the way down the hall into the main living area. "Your room is just how you left it."

"Thanks," Eren replied, stealing a glance through the guest room doorway. Her *Tron* movie poster—a gift from the theater manager in Brookings who'd had a major crush on her —still hung on the wall over the twin bed in the corner. "I hope you've been taking good care of my car."

Liam laughed aloud. "*Your* car? Um, Wendy...darling...light of my life..." Eren loved *The Shining*, and Liam had missed quoting lines to her. "I do believe you signed the pink slip over to me."

He handed her a Coke from the fridge, and she snapped open the tab with that deeply satisfying sound of pressure released. "True story. But come on, I gave it to you in cherry condition."

"It's still cherry," Liam assured her, offering his can in a toast, which she answered with her own. The two cans met with a dull aluminum *clunk*. "And I'm working at the shop, so I get parts wholesale. Free, if I can pick 'em off a wreck."

Their reunion consisted of soda, sharing the joint Liam had previously been rolling, and deep conversation until 3 a.m. Liam filled her in on the surveillance and tailing by the feds—presumably from a reactivated Project Black Eagle, or at least that was his theory. Eren pretty much confirmed it with her silence. He told her about Deputy Pete Halverson's alleged scandal and apparent suicide, and that seemed to elicit a genuine look of sadness from his visitor.

In turn, Eren updated Liam with the important points of her current mission. It was agreed she should make her pitch to the group the following morning, after a more public appearance at the diner. It would arouse less suspicion, as Eren was anything but low-profile in Calico.

Finally Liam wandered to his bedroom and collapsed on the unmade bed, nudging the door shut with his foot. Eren trundled off to the third bedroom, unused since her departure almost a year ago, just as Liam had promised.

Halfway down the block, the mysterious black Ford sedan sat quietly parked, four silhouetted figures inside. They were completely silent, and completely still.

◌⊰

There was nobody.

No *body* at all. Or *bodies*, rather.

By the time the sheriff arrived, another Bronco was already parked at the scene, a couple of Curry County deputies scanning the edge of the road with flashlights. One of them had a sable-colored German shepherd on a short lead.

Exiting her own vehicle, Chavez ran the beam of her police Maglite across the gravel and dirt between the abandoned vehicles and where the logging spur met the forest's edge, tracing a dark, bloodstained trail.

Neither car appeared disabled, both sets of keys still in their respective ignitions. But the scene was a crimson mess. Blood on the driver's seat of Mary Grisham's station wagon. Blood on the front bumper and grille. Blood in a large, circular stain in front of Butch Carlton's pickup.

Reaching through the open driver's side door in the rusted Chevy truck, she nudged open the cooler on the front bench seat with the butt of her flashlight. It was full of trout and one impressive salmon, all untouched.

"What the hell happened here?" she wondered aloud, which drew the attention of Deputy Lewis from the dirt road.

"Ma'am?"

Chavez took a breath, but it didn't help to calm her. "You run the plates?"

"Yeah," Lewis responded, consulting a small notepad. "The truck is registered to a Butch Carlton, the wagon to Mary Grisham."

Chavez squinted across the river to the sparkling lights of Calico. She didn't know Butch personally, but she'd shopped at Mary's grocery store in the past. "I don't get any of this, Lewis."

The tall deputy shuffled a well-worn boot in the dirt. "Looks like maybe the driver of the Chevy pulled up to help the driver of the wagon, and they were attacked?"

"Attacked?"

"Most likely an animal of some kind."

Chavez looked dubious. "Like what?"

"Y'all got wolves up here?"

"Ever heard of a wolf pack hunting this close to the coast?"

"No, ma'am. California hasn't had any since the 1920s."

Chavez pursed her lips, imagining settlers indiscriminately slaughtering entire packs to ensure the safety of their livestock. "Well we still have some, and they don't range this far. Nearest one we know is down near Medford."

Lewis thumbed the cap back on his shaved head. "Cougar, maybe?"

"Cougars," Chavez explained, "are solitary hunters—not likely a single cat could have taken down two adult humans and dragged them off that far. And we're not usually on their menu." She gestured at the cooler in the truck. "Even if something was attracted by the fish, whatever did this left the actual food source alone, and didn't damage the vehicles."

Lewis rested a muscular hand on his gun belt. "Well, I'm just about all out of ideas, ma'am. If it's not an animal predator, then we're looking at—"

"A human," Chavez finished. "Until we know for sure, Mary Grisham and Butch Carlton are *missing*. But we need to be prepared for this to become a double homicide really damn quickly."

As if on cue, the second deputy cried out from where the road disappeared into the woods. "Hey Lewis! Sheriff! I got bodies!"

Chavez threw Lewis a knowing glance. "Get photos and bag 'em up. I'll get the Medical Examiner's office in on the case." As he turned to step away, she caught his arm and added: "But keep this as quiet as you can—no reporters."

The deputy nodded, meeting her gaze. "No reporters. You got it, ma'am."

ଓ

The Friday morning breakfast rush was slow. Despite the Silver City Diner's central location and no shortage of students on summer break, there were mornings—especially weekdays—when the locals just didn't bother to show up early. The Korolewskis had run the place long enough to know the ebbs and flows of their clientele, and their associated feeding habits, so no one was particularly worried. Sometimes during the summer, the cannery workers who would ordinarily be there to scarf down a couple of fried eggs before a shift would opt to take their families on long weekends up the coast to the Tillamook Creamery or the Sea Lion Caves, or down the coast to Crescent City in Northern California.

At least they could always depend on the lunch rush.

Lori Tran was already nursing a cup of coffee at her favorite table when Chlöe entered, emanating petulance in her daily countdown until Bodhi's return. Molly trailed in after her, rolling her eyes like the expert teenager she was. Her reprieve from Chlöe's unusually abrasive attitude was to steal a kiss from Kris as he wiped down a table with a lemon-scented dish towel. Though he was focused on his work, Molly saw the left side of his mouth creep up into the hint of a smile, and that was all the validation she needed.

Chlöe pouted, sure that Molly had done it on purpose just to spite the fact that her own boyfriend was still gallivanting across Germany, probably meeting all sorts of sexy young European girls, and...oh hell. She had to find a diversion from counting the hours until their reunion. This was not healthy. She knew it wasn't. And then there was the whole "boyfriend" thing. That was yet another problem, because they weren't *actually currently* dating. They had decided to take a break during the school year, since Bodhi was going to college at UCLA, and Chlöe was a junior at Calico High. She had one more year before they could even be in the same city, outside of Bodhi visiting home over the summer, Spring Break or the holidays. She *really* needed to be distracted, because her tendency of overthinking was starting to manifest in all sorts of bizarre, anti-social ways, and her friends were definitely beginning to notice.

Lori took in the scene with an air of detached interest, as if observing gorillas in the wild. She scribbled in a small notepad. Not her anthropological notes, but a verse of observational poetry she imagined singing on a stage with her as-yet nonexistent goth band, Sclera. She took notice, however, when A.J. and Liam entered in the company of a gorgeous, green-haired girl in a black leather jacket. She couldn't tell if she was attracted to the stranger, hated her, or was just jealous of her wardrobe. Perhaps a little of all three?

Judging from the concert tee, she clearly liked Killing Joke, so hating her was probably out of the question. Lori had hoped to talk to A.J. today, and perhaps ask him out (if he didn't do it first), and if there was something between him and this girl...woman...

Not so fast, Lori, she thought. *You're getting out over your skis. Just wait for some context.*

The first five minutes of Eren's arrival at the diner was a solid pantomime of jaws hitting the floor, elated cries and warm embraces. Even Kris managed to sneak away from busing tables to join the tiny crowd around Eren. Six teenagers crammed into the family booth—which had a capacity for eight—and the grilling began.

"Eren, how have you been?"

"What's been going on?"

"What brings you back to Calico?"

"Oh my *gawd*, I love your hair!"

Eren basked in the glow of her friends' adoration, exchanging pleasantries with each of them in turn, finally steering the conversation away from her and onto the goings on within the group. She'd already had an update from the prior night's visits with A.J. and Liam, but the others didn't know that, and they were excited to fill her in all over again.

In the midst of Kris spinning a recap of their recent roleplaying adventures, Eren gave A.J. a soft nudge in the ribs. "Is that Lori?" she whispered, nodding toward the girl at the corner table—the girl who was trying to observe without *looking* like she was observing.

A.J. glanced over and blushed immediately. "Yeah."

"Dude, you're missing it," Eren chuckled in his ear. "She's totally into you."

Another flare of red cheeks, and A.J. cleared his throat. "So, um, what did you think of the story?"

Eren drew her lips into a smile, allowing A.J. to wriggle off the hook for the time being.

"I loved it. Those are characters from our *D&D* campaign last year, right?"

As A.J. nodded, Kris stood from the outside spot on the curved seat and leveled an accusatory finger at him. "Yeah, except my character didn't die like a punk in our campaign."

"Relax, Kris," Eren said calmly. "It's a little thing called *artistic license*. A.J.'s a storyteller. Just because this version is different from the one we played, doesn't make it better or worse."

Of course, Kris knew all of that. He just didn't like the idea of letting his best friend live something down without the requisite amount of good-natured grief. "I know, I know," he admitted, backing away to finish his shift. "But you're still a rat bastard, Alan Jennings."

A.J. smiled, pointing back at him. "I am a tenth level bard, you pathetic pile of orc droppings!"

"Oh, well played," Eren sighed, once again nodding in the direction of Lori Tran.

Before A.J. had time to register the effect of his nerdy display, Eren refocused the conversation.

"So are Chlöe and Bodhi still a thing?"

Chlöe clenched her teeth, but managed to blurt something out relating to her college applications including UCLA, and how she and Bodhi had been taking a break, but that there would definitely be a discussion when he returned from abroad.

Eren nodded along, but found Chlöe especially hard to read.

"And you and Kris?" Eren turned to Molly with a jovial grin. "How long has this been going on?"

Molly blushed into her mug of cocoa.

"Long enough," A.J. muttered.

Liam chuckled through a Billy Idol snarl. "That's what your mom said."

All three of the female persuasion rolled their eyes at the juvenile quip, but it was only performative. They were just jealous none of them had said it first.

"I was hoping we could meet," Eren said with a look of sudden, serious intent. "I have something I need to discuss with the group."

A.J. frowned. He knew what this was about, and he wasn't exactly looking forward to the discussion. "I have to work noon to four. But tonight maybe?"

"At our place," Molly suggested. "The folks are down in Grant's Pass again. We'll have the rec room to ourselves."

Eren stood from the booth, leaning her hands on the table. "Tonight then. I'm gonna go take care of some errands. See you at the Casa de Reynolds."

A.J. slid out to let Liam follow her, as he was her ride. Kris made some comment about "Eren running *erens*", but she didn't seem to hear. As A.J. watched, she sauntered over to Lori's table, said something in a low tone with a smile, crossing to exit the diner with Liam.

Lori Tran scribbled away in her notebook, stealing the occasional furtive glance at A.J.'s booth.

Track 13:

I SCARE MYSELF

Thomas Dolby (1984)

The rare sight of police lights and wail of sirens pierced the late morning calm over Calico, as two ambulances, escorted by a lone Sheriff's Department Bronco, roared down the North Bank frontage road toward Wedderburn. There was a momentary flurry of interest, as folks looked up from their newspapers or peered out of their office windows—not that they could actually see the road from most venues in town.

A few cannery workers on a smoke break during their morning shift were able to watch the vehicles pass, steering the conversation toward the fact that *two ambulances meant something really bad, like maybe a car turned over at Salmon Creek Bridge, and what did it have to do with Deputy Halverson's suicide...? Nothing, Carl, you idiot—why do you always connect everything to the latest news event?*

A.J. gathered the finished set of photo prints from the tray of the drugstore mini-lab and slid them into the printed envelope with the customer's contact info scrawled on the outside. Colleen Hempler, a P.E. teacher at the Junior High, had found a missing film canister from a ski trip to Mt. Bachelor with her boyfriend back in January.

He was filing the envelope in the drawer under H when a familiar face, framed in teased black hair, approached the photo counter.

"So, that girl..." Lori Tran offered with almost comical nonchalance.

A.J. squinted through his glasses. "Oh, hey Lori." Clearing his throat, he queried back: "Uh, girl?"

"At the diner this morning?" Lori prodded. "Tall, tan, amazing green hair?"

Immediately, A.J. knew what this was about. He needed to set the record straight in a quick and simple manner. "Eren? Oh, she's Liam's cousin, out visiting from Montana. She was living here with Liam and his mom last year, until school started in the fall." He caught himself before going into the story about her being an interdimensional traveler who had enlisted their help to steal a spaceship back from the United States government and defend an alternate Earth against an invading alien force. Still, he wondered if his meager explanation wasn't a bit *too* casual—and thereby over-selling.

He blinked, inhaling the scent of cloves that lingered on her black cardigan. Damn, she smelled good.

Lori paused, lips pursed in thought. "Hmm. Okay, then." And just like that, after weeks of inner debate, throughout the final quarter of the school year, she came to a conclusion. "So, were you gonna wait until summer was over to ask me out, or what?"

A.J. had been to an alternate universe, and had teleported within his own. He'd seen ghosts numbering in the hundreds, and had closed a dimensional portal while dressed as Rick Deckard from *Blade Runner*. But matters of the heart were beyond his realm of imagination. He felt like a baby deer finding its legs for the first time. "I...was gonna do that, um...today. Now. Right now." He recalled the same feeling from a couple of days previous, when she'd grilled him on his favorite bands. It was slightly uncomfortable, being put on the spot like that, being made the focus. But it wasn't altogether horrible—in fact, he was growing to like it. Someone who could keep him on his toes meant she was an intellectual equal, and he found that *extremely* attractive.

Lori cracked a wry smile. She could read the internal battle written on his face. "Right now, huh?"

Pull yourself together, Jenkins, A.J. thought, assembling his next words in the correct order. "Yeah, uh, you wanna go see a movie, maybe grab some food? That new movie *Ghostbusters* just opened last week, and I've been waiting for the right Asian goth chick to go with."

"What a coincidence," Lori winked. "I've been waiting for the right nerdy white boy to take me to see it. Plus, I loved Sigourney Weaver in *Alien.* Can't wait to see what she does with a comedy." A pause developed as each tried to work their own mental day planner.

"Did you mean tonight?" Lori asked.

A.J. balked. "Um, no. Sorry. I have...a prior commitment."

"So tomorrow, then?"

"Cool. I have to work in the morning, but if I can get ahead of the photo processing, I can be out by one or so."

"Wow, you can just set your schedule like that?"

"My mom's the manager," A.J. shrugged with a sheepish grin.

Lori chuckled softly. "Cushy."

"I think there's a four o'clock show at the Redwood Theater in Brookings. We can get dinner after?"

"Sounds good. You wanna pick me up?"

A.J. ran through the logistics. Riding bikes was always an option for a couple kids going on a harmless local date, but he preferred the status and comfort of being in a car, and Brookings was thirty-plus miles distant. But there was a key element missing. "I won't have my license until August," he admitted.

Lori was unfazed. "That's okay. I'll pick you up." She opened her notebook and set it on the counter, turning it toward him.

A.J. stared at the open book, momentarily clueless. This was new territory. What was happening here? Did she want him to read her poetry?

"Address and phone number," she instructed. "Or I can just pick you up here."

He grabbed a ballpoint pen from his apron pocket and scribbled down the relevant information. "Here you go. Say three?"

"Three it is. Smell you later."

As he watched Lori delicately close the notebook and exit the store, his initial giddiness turned to dread. Dread at the realization that he was now going to have to juggle his summer work schedule, a budding romance, and whatever Eren had planned. And he had to keep Lori separate from anything related to Eren and her dimension-hopping mission, saving whoever remained of the first crew, and the feds increasing their surveillance and intimidation.

He really didn't want to drag her into that mess. It wasn't the best environment for a new relationship—his first relationship—to say the least.

At four o'clock, A.J. waved a casual farewell to his mother, mentioned he was going to hang out at Molly's place, but he wouldn't be out too late. She reminded him of his early shift the following morning, and he offered a casual thumbs up in response as he exited through the glass doors.

Moving to unlock his bicycle from the rack in front of the drugstore, he glanced across the street and noticed a familiar black sedan parked facing 2nd Avenue. With surprising grace born of muscle memory, A.J. saddled up and pedaled onto 3rd Avenue, away from the mystery car. He took a circuitous route toward home, checking behind himself every so often to make sure the vehicle wasn't tailing him. Thinking for a moment that he might be paranoid, he remembered that he and his friends had literally busted an interdimensional spaceship out of federal custody, so no amount of paranoia was actually unjustified.

He began to breathe a bit easier as he leaned into the right curve on upper Ash Street. Arriving at home with no further sighting of the black Ford, A.J. retreated to his room to wait for Liam and Eren to fetch him for the meeting.

The summer was about to get significantly more dangerous. And so much weirder.

☙

Sheriff Chavez sipped from a tall ceramic coffee mug as she inventoried the tower of file folders stacked on her desk. The Grisham and Carlton homicides at the logging spur. The four dead bodies brought in that morning, apparently after being discovered in a parked Ford sedan by a local resident while he was jogging.

For a community which for decades could boast a murder record of precisely zero, to suddenly have six within twenty-four hours—not including a rather fishy suicide—was extremely troubling.

Pulling a folder from the bottom of the pile, she flipped open the one with the most personal connection—Deputy Pete Halverson.

From a locked drawer in her desk, she drew the other folder Pete had hidden inside his barbecue grill. The first archive was full of evidence meant to incriminate Halverson with all manner of unsavory (and frankly unbelievable) activities he was alleged to have done. The second was the evidence he'd collected over a year of investigating a mysterious crash site, a shadowy government organization, and its secret facility in the deep woods.

Thumbing through the documents in the first, she ran across some photos of Halverson apparently entering a California motel with a teenage girl whose face was obscured.

She sighed, taking another sip of strong coffee, before she noticed the time stamp embedded on the photo print. Her face froze in mid-swallow.

Hold on just a minute.

Standing bolt upright from her office chair, Chavez strode to the door. Deputy Mike Lewis was standing in the hall outside, just about to knock.

"Oh, uh, morning, Sheriff."

Chavez looked past him. "Come with me," she ordered, slapping his broad shoulder with the incriminating photo.

He followed her across the hall to the office he used to share with Halverson before it became his alone. "Ma'am?"

"Wednesday, December 29th, 1982," she answered, heading directly to the metal filing cabinet next to Pete's former desk.

Lewis followed her, confused. "That was before my time, ma'am."

Chavez hauled open the middle drawer and began flipping through the rows of folders within. "It happened in late December '82...the file should be in here somewhere."

Lewis cast a quizzical look at the floor. "December 29th, 1982?"

"Yes," Chevez answered, continuing to paw through the line of file folders. "I remember we were out at the crash site."

"Crash site?" Lewis wondered. "Ma'am?"

"He wrote up a report that night. Here it is."

A chill shot up her spine as her finger brushed over the label on the folder: BLACK EAGLE. She ripped it from the drawer and slapped it open on the empty desk, rifling through its contents. It mostly consisted of early photographs of the crash site of Eren's power core, as well as a collection of duty logs and reports. Something among them caught her eye.

"There," she said breathlessly, pointing out the date entry on one report in particular. "December 29th, 1982. An object of unknown origin had crashed out east of Jerry's Flat Road. It made a lot of noise and an impact trough almost a hundred feet long. There were lots of witnesses there. We were both at the site, and I can verify it with my own daily log."

Lewis was no less confused than before. "Sheriff? What's the deal?"

Chavez finally realized she hadn't let Lewis in on the story. "Pete Halverson couldn't have been in California that day. He was on duty, with me. Half of Calico and Gold Beach witnessed him there. He's the victim of a set up."

"Set up?" Lewis puzzled. "Set up by who? For what purpose?"

"By some unknown agency of the federal government, probably to draw us off investigating that crash site, and their related activities. And maybe as reprisal for snooping around in the first place."

"How much snooping around could he have done?"

"I'm not *exactly* sure," Chavez mused, shutting the file and tucking it under her arm. "It was a pet project of his. He spent a lot of his off-hours looking into it. I know he mentioned finding what looked like a military facility in the deep woods, though he also said it appeared abandoned. Regardless, I have a bunch of photos he took that corroborate his story. Photos he was hiding from prying eyes."

Then she remembered that A.J. and Liam and their gang had also been at the crash site that day, and that Liam seemed to have a vested interest in Halverson's fate. The more she thought about it, the more she realized that they'd been at the center of a host of unusual situations in and around Calico in the '82, '83 time frame.

"Lewis," she addressed the deputy in a low tone, "where were those four bodies found this morning? The ones in the parked sedan?"

Lewis folded his arms across a sinewy chest. "I'd have to check to make sure," he offered, "but I think it was out at the east side of town...West Evergreen?"

"Amber Scott lives on West Evergreen," she sighed.

"The lady we just had in here sleeping off a bender?"

Chavez turned to regard Lewis in a professorial manner. "The single mother of Liam Scott, the boy who drives that black El Camino and hangs out with Jenkins and Korolewski and the Reynolds kids. I want you to keep an eye on them," she said. "And keep this conversation under your hat."

"Mum's the word, Sheriff."

Mike Lewis pursed his lips in a confused circle as a realization dawned on him. He'd need more detail, of course, but in the context of a single conversation, Chavez was clearly indicating that the aforementioned kids, members of the Curry County Sheriff's Department, and perhaps even the entire town of Calico, Oregon could all be in serious danger.

Track 14:
TURN TO YOU
The Go-Go's (1984)

A.J., Eren, and Liam found the rest of the gang in the basement rec room as always, and it filled all three of them with an easy sense of comfort and continuity. Chlöe sat snuggled with a throw pillow at one end of the old sofa, while Molly and Kris shot a round of pool and made small talk. The color television on the plastic rolling cart in the corner played a classic creature feature with the sound off— a man in a rubber *kaiju* suit trampled a scale model of Tokyo while citizens screamed in terror and pointed at the sky. Considering how quickly the teen years seemed to pass, this was a surprisingly static tableau.

Same as it ever was, Eren thought, quoting the Talking Heads. And yet tonight was a different animal somehow.

"There they are," Chlöe observed from the corner of the couch.

Kris grinned as he lined up a shot on the table. "The return of Space Commander Eren!"

"A bit reductive," A.J. quipped as he tossed his backpack gently at the foot of the empty recliner. "Don't you think?"

"Sounds better than Dimension Commander Eren," Molly retorted.

Liam went to the fridge for a can of soda. "Come on, guys. Space-*time* Commander Eren. It writes itself."

"You guys are still hilarious," Eren sighed, leaning against the side of the pool table as Molly and Kris put their sticks in the wall rack and went to claim the other half of the sofa.

"Are you surprised?" Molly chuckled.

Eren leaned forward and winked at her. "Not at all. In fact I think that's why we always got along so well."

"You mean our ability to employ gallows humor under extreme duress?" A.J. was only half joking, and his tone told everyone he knew what was going on. At least to a greater degree than the rest of them.

"Uh oh," Kris muttered. "Here it comes."

The group trained their collective eyes on Eren, and for the first time since her initial introduction, she felt nervous. The kind of nervous that came with full-on nausea and a side of anxiety. "Okay, first off, I need you all to give me a super-double-secret pinky swear of total confidence. Mostly for your own safety." Her eyes blazed with intensity. "I don't need Chavez or the local cops getting involved, and I certainly don't want the feds to come sniffing around."

"Too late," Liam observed.

Eren sighed. "Fair."

"You have our most solemn vow of discretion," A.J. assured her, earning several confused looks from the trio on the couch.

Molly squinted at her. "Eren. What is it?"

"Well," Eren continued, "as I told Liam and A.J. last night, I'm here to bring home the survivors from the recovery team."

"Recovery team?" Kris wondered.

Liam turned the soda can in both hands. "The first travelers, who ditched the weapon in our dimension, got caught and are presumed dead. The recovery team was sent to retrieve the weapon and bring it home—what we ended up doing. They got caught too."

"I thought they were dead," Chlöe frowned. "Or vanished into Area 51 or whatever."

Eren nodded. "That's what we thought. We also thought Project Black Eagle was mothballed, and that's clearly not the case. Long story short, three of the recovery team escaped and managed to get a message back. They're hiding out in the woods somewhere in the Siskiyou Forest, and I want to find them before anyone else—feds, local law enforcement, the media…"

"Rednecks," Liam added.

"Rednecks for sure. Anyway, all I know is that they're out there in almost thousands of square miles of wilderness, and the feds are already sniffing around. They're branded for travel, but they've never been inside the ship I brought through, and they have no idea where it's parked. So we'll have to make physical contact to be able to teleport."

Molly raised her hand out of habit. "We should put glyphs in everyone's homes."

"Can do," Eren said softly, eyes beginning to rim with tears.

"And the El Camino," Liam suggested.

Eren cocked her head. "Interesting thought. I've never branded a vehicle…I mean, our ships have them built in. But I've never jumped through a moving gate. We might have to test it out."

"What kind of supplies do they have?" Molly wondered. "Like, how long do you think they can stay out there?"

"No clue. We don't know when they actually broke out of custody. They're all trained in wilderness survival, but they can't last forever."

Liam scratched his temple, deep in what passed for thought. "Seems like they might have kyped some tech gear when they escaped. If they were able to send a distress call home."

"Correct," Eren admitted, "I went to the coordinates and found some discarded components."

A.J. had a sudden concern. "Um, hang on. The recovery team...didn't they place the original portals around Old Town? Why didn't they just blink back to one of them? The old mines are a prime spot to hide out in. Would've made them easier to find." Realizing he'd just answered his own question, he sighed, relaxing back into the chair. "Nevermind. I see it now."

"What?" Chlöe wondered. "What do you see now?"

"We have to assume the feds already know about the portals at Old Town. Even if they don't know how to operate them. If the recovery team would be easier for us to find, they'd also be easier for the feds to find."

"So what's the plan?" Kris asked, and Eren took a moment to find each person's eyes.

"That sounds like you're in?"

"I told you," A.J. huffed. "We're all in. You just needed to ask."

"Thank you," she said, holding back a towering wave of emotion behind a stoic facade. "The plan is to search in a grid, leaving glyphs every so often so we can minimize travel time. But that means..."

"Phantoms," Kris finished.

"Phantoms," repeated Eren, nodding in quiet resignation. "I wish it wasn't the case, but we're going to be doing a lot of jumping, and that means an increase in phantoms in the vicinity of our work. Fortunately, we'll mostly be in the deep woods, so we won't need to manage them in a public setting."

"We've done that already," Liam boasted, pointing finger guns in her direction. "Ain't no big thang."

"No doubt," Molly boasted, raising her hand again, for a different reason. "Up high."

Kris met her gesture and they slapped hands, then he had a sudden thought.

"Is anyone concerned," Kris asked the group, "that A.J. saw that recent ghost without the aid of *babciu's* pumpkin cookies?"

Liam shrugged. "Remember, we saw a bunch of phantoms out in Old Town that first time. We didn't have the cookies then."

"Could have been close proximity to a couple of portals in the local area," A.J. posed. "If appearing to the naked eye takes more energy, maybe they had it to spare."

"It shouldn't make a difference," Eren pressed on. "We know how to protect ourselves. Just don't become unconscious around them." The group nodded in unison. "The first thing I need to do is take you out to the ship, so you can jump back there if you locate one of the lost crew. Any problem with going tomorrow?"

"I'm cool with that," Kris offered, but A.J. was already clearing his throat.

"I can't do tomorrow," he explained. "Got a morning shift at the drug store, and...I...sort of...have a date."

The group suddenly shifted its collective focus to A.J., and he instantly regretted saying anything.

"The goth chick from the diner?" Eren smiled, raising an eyebrow.

A.J. pressed his lips together, resembling a Muppet. "Yeah. Lori."

"Holy shit!" Kris and Molly exclaimed in unison.

Chlöe grinned, nodding motherly encouragement. "Right on."

"Dude," Liam chided. "Reschedule. This is important. You're on the clock here, buddy."

"No," Eren said firmly, standing with arms folded. "None of you are on the clock. This is *my* mission, and you've already done so much. For me. For my world." She slowly moved to where A.J. sat in the recliner, staring at his shoes. "Your lives are important," she said, stroking his hair with a gentle touch. "You need to live them."

"Well what about Sunday?" Liam proposed, his words dripping sarcasm. "Do you have a date on Sunday?"

A.J. opened his writing notebook and peered over his glasses. "Let me just check my social calendar...hmmm...let's see. Yes, I think I can do Sunday." He pretended to write in the book, adding, "Rescue...interdimensional...fugitives."

That drew a collective chuckle from the group, and Eren rested a hand on A.J.'s shoulder as she regarded them. "That's my tribe."

CB

Sheriff Chavez locked her file drawer and was packing up for the day when Deputy Lewis appeared in her office. Giving a perfunctory knock on the open door frame, he craned his neck into the tiny room.

"Sheriff, I think you should be aware..."

Chavez squinted, bearing in mind their earlier exchange that day. "What is it, Lewis?"

"Feds, ma'am. I just got a call from the M.E. They showed up at Curry General and took the bodies that came in from Calico this morning."

"—the hell?" Chavez bristled, stepping around her desk to get to the door. "I ordered autopsies!"

"I know, ma'am."

"When did this happen?"

"Just now," Lewis explained. "Within five, ten minutes."

While she understood that Pete Halverson had somehow run afoul of whichever federal agency and some unspoken rule of investigation and/or jurisdiction, this degree of meddling was beginning to stick in her craw. And if she was right in her assumption that Pete hadn't killed himself, well...assassination of local law enforcement was some CIA-level black-ops shit, squarely outside of any official law, and with zero recourse.

And it wasn't like she could file a report with the FBI. Calling the feds on the feds? Useless, at best. The situation was rapidly spiraling out of control. She had to circle the wagons as best she could, at the very least to protect her department and its deputies from further reprisal. If they could murder a sheriff's deputy and stage it as a suicide, complete with incriminating "evidence" of unsavory activities, then she knew they'd be willing to go much further—as far as necessary to keep their little science project a secret.

Lewis was already clued in, but nobody else was going to be put in danger because of the information she was privy to. She'd make do with Deputy Lewis. He was a good officer, with a history of standing up to authority where necessary, and speaking truth to power. It was one of the reasons she'd taken him when he left the Siskiyou County Sheriff's Department in California.

"*Mierda*," Chavez cursed under her breath. "Okay, you're with me. Come on."

They headed to Curry General in the sheriff's Bronco, arriving too late to intercept the agents absconding with her corpses, and getting a bewildered narrative from the medical examiner who'd been prepping the autopsies.

Doctor Ted Bollinger was a thrice-divorced alcoholic with undiagnosed depression, but he was never impaired on the job, nor was he prone to wild speculation or tall tales. He included physical descriptions of the agents who invaded his morgue not fifteen minutes previous, and detailed their actions—which included destroying his initial written records and opening his camera to rip out the film, exposing the shots he'd already taken.

There were four men and two women, all in dark suits, sunglasses, and audio earpieces. They were quick, efficient, and only one of them spoke. "Tall fella, dark hair slicked back, Tom Selleck mustache. Had some pock marks on his cheeks, probably acne scarring. He seemed to be the one in charge."

Chavez nodded along as Lewis scribbled notes in his pad.

"What did he say?" she asked.

Bollinger shrugged. "Like I say, not much. They sorta swooped in, put the bodies on gurneys, took my notes, tore out my film. The tall fella, he says, 'Thanks—we'll take it from here. No need to follow up.' And he addressed me by name."

"Did you challenge their authority?"

"Hell no. Six of them, and one of me. They're all packing sidearms under their jackets, and all I've got is a bone saw. Besides, I know feds when I see 'em. Trust me when I say I've been around the block. I served in 'Nam from '65 to '69, and I know what my government is capable of. I just wanna do my job and go home at night. But I thought the Curry

County Sheriff should at least be aware of the goings on around here."

"Understood," Chavez sighed, clapping a friendly hand on Bollinger's shoulder. "Did they do anything with Pete Halverson's body?"

"Nope. He's still in freezer seven."

"And you still think he was a suicide?"

"Not at all. Never did." The examiner produced a ballpoint pen from the chest pocket of his lab coat, pointing at the center of his brow with the closed end. "Nobody shoots themselves in the head from that degree of elevation. Not a natural position."

"But the report. You signed off—"

"Yeah, that's my signature on the report. Someone higher up the food chain wanted it to be a suicide. I'm telling you, in my professional opinion, it wasn't."

Chavez paused, running her tongue thoughtfully inside closed lips. "Is there anything else you can tell us?"

"Well, yeah," Bollinger frowned, using the pen to scratch at a receding gray hairline. "The bodies they took—I assume they were fellow agents, given their clothing. Same dark suits and all. But what's got me confused is that they were so focused on erasing all evidence of those four that they completely ignored the other two in the freezer."

Chavez blinked, glancing over at Lewis.

"Carlton and Grisham," the deputy stated, eyes growing wide.

"Are they still here?" Chavez wondered.

Dr. Bollinger pointed at a bank of eight freezers used for storing dead bodies for autopsy or transfer to the local funeral home. "Sure. Right there, in number two and number three."

Chavez went to freezer three and pulled the release, sliding the metal slab outward to reveal a semi-opaque white body bag, zipped down the middle. Lewis lowered the zipper enough to expose the pale, dead face of Mary Grisham, eyes open and gauzy white.

"Thing is," the doctor continued, "those two died in the same manner as the agents in the car, near as I can figure."

"How so?" Lewis asked.

Bollinger joined them over the corpse, pen still in hand. He gently opened more of the body bag and proceeded to point out various features of Mary's wounds. "On the surface, it looks like an animal attack. See here, around the collar bone. But the wound that caused exsanguination and death is over here, around to the side of the neck, at the carotid artery. It's circular, with multiple small punctures, almost like a leech if you scaled it up to the size of an adult human."

Chavez and Lewis exchanged a silent look.

"And the four agents? They had the same wounds?"

"Identical," the doctor replied. "It's in my report on these two." Bollinger shuffled to the office adjacent to the morgue, where he opened a file drawer and pulled two folders from within. Chavez met him at the office door, and he slapped the files into her arms.

"Has anyone else seen these reports?"

Bollinger mused for a moment, recalling dates and times. "Now, they came in Thursday night, I did the exam on Friday, but the State and County copies won't be filed until Monday. Did you want me to hold onto them?"

Chavez flirted with the idea to have him misplace the reports for a week or so, just to let her get caught up. But then it dawned on her that anything her office did to obscure evidence from official review would only play into the hands of whatever shadowy agency they were dealing with. This wasn't investigation or law enforcement. This was more like internal espionage.

"No," she instructed. "Don't do anything differently in terms of filing the reports, but I'd like to have a copy, for our ongoing investigation."

Dr. Bollinger nodded at the folders in her hand. "Take them. And Godspeed, Sheriff. If you—or any of us—run afoul of these people, or whatever it was that killed Carlton and Grisham, it ain't gonna be pretty."

Track 15:
I WILL DARE
The Replacements (1984)

Saturday morning brought the crisp scent of pine through A.J.'s bedroom window. He woke with a smile and proceeded to the bathroom, where he scrubbed his entire person from head to toe. Although he'd been using deodorant for the past couple of years, A.J. gave himself a double application in each armpit. His entire wardrobe was clean from the dresser, from the white cotton chinos to the navy blue polo shirt, his basic work uniform.

He spent almost fifteen minutes conversing with his parents in the kitchen, which bewildered and amused mom and dad both. They chatted about his summer plans as he worked his way through a bowl of Honey Nut Cheerios while leaning against the counter, then he zipped up a gray hoodie and headed out to his bike.

A singular lightness infected his every step, every move, every rotation of bike pedals, as he swerved his way across town to the Val-U-Drug on 3rd and Union. It was almost like an alcohol buzz—a ridiculous excitement filled with both uncertainty and ego. A girl—not just any random girl, but someone he'd crushed on from afar—seemed legitimately interested in him. He was going to see her, ride in her car, and sit next to her in a darkened theater. And then they were going to sit across from one another and talk about movies and music and art, and stare into each other's eyes. And all he had to do was get through his shift, get back home, and change clothes before 3 p.m. without having a complete mental breakdown.

Easy as pie.

But the day did not cooperate. He arrived to discover whoever had closed the night before had left a photo job to run with the wrong settings on the Autolab, and every print was black. He had to chuck the photos in the trash, recalibrate the machine, and re-run the order. A.J. was stuffing the new prints in the envelope just as old Mrs. Bryce arrived to pick them up. You didn't get between Mrs. Bryce and twenty-four photos of her granddaughter's 4th birthday party. Not ever.

The rest of the shift dragged on interminably, with perhaps four customers at the photo counter, all to pick up. At noon, a fifth wandered in for a set of passport pictures, which took all of six minutes. A.J. watched the wall clock with the apprehension of an inmate waiting for the parole meeting to start.

Finally, after a perceived ice age, the clock admitted it was 1 p.m., and A.J. bolted. He'd had the photo area organized and tidy since 12:30.

Less than fifteen minutes for the ride home, then a quick change of wardrobe consisting of faded Levi's and a black Joy Division t-shirt. While the shirt design didn't actually *say* "Joy Division", it displayed the stacked plot of pulsar radio waves in a graphic design adopted by the band for their first album, *Unknown Pleasures*. In the years since frontman Ian Curtis' suicide, the design had become a logo of sorts. A shorthand among alternative music fans. A secret handshake for the club.

A.J. brushed his teeth again to purge the taste of the deli sandwich he'd grabbed for lunch. It was churning in his stomach and making vague threats, but A.J. promised himself some pizza from Gizmo's later, and that seemed to settle things a bit. The gray hoodie went back on, unzipped low enough so that the wavy white pulsar lines on the shirt were visible. He wasn't going to go through the effort of wearing the secret handshake and not actually *give* the secret handshake, after all.

And then he waited.

At 2:56 p.m., Lori pulled up to the Jenkins house in a maroon 1978 Datsun B210 GX. A.J. wasn't sure what he'd expected. A jet black hearse, maybe.

"Nice ride," he muttered as he slid onto the passenger seat. The interior smelled of cloves and sandalwood incense, and was decorated in plastic skulls and spiders, the cracked dashboard seemingly held together with various radio station and rock band stickers.

Lori wore a variation on her usual theme: baggy black cardigan with the sleeves pushed up to the elbows to display a collection of plastic and metal bangles and a studded leather wristband, a Siouxsie & The Banshees concert tee, red plaid miniskirt with black fishnets, and—of course—black Doc Marten boots. Her eyes were done up in a heavy Egyptian style that accentuated their natural shape. Lips were a shade somewhere between crime scene blood spatter and charcoal. An assortment of silver rings encircled several fingers and dangled from both ears, and her hair was teased into a ratty mop, held in place with a black plastic hairband and half a can of Aqua Net.

"Nice shirt," she remarked, catching a glimpse of the pulsar waves scrawled across

A.J.'s chest. "If I didn't already know you were cool, I'd think you were a poser."

She thinks I'm cool!

"Good thing you know better," he quipped, nodding at her own wardrobe. "And you're looking super gothy today."

Lori smirked, peering over a pair of imitation Ray Ban sunglasses. "Oh this? This isn't *super* gothy. You'd know if I was going for *super* goth."

"Okay," A.J. laughed. "*Demi-goth* then."

Lori looked to the road and shifted into gear. "Demi-goth," she repeated with a grin. "I like it."

It was 32 miles to Brookings, another coastal Oregon town just south of Gold Beach by way of Highway 101 along the coast. On the drive, they rocked out to the mix tape in Lori's stereo, and A.J. realized she was every bit Molly's equal in her selection and editing. It was an eclectic assortment of older tracks from art rock bands like Shocking Blue, Iggy & the Stooges, and The Velvet Underground, interspersed with more recent fare from Cocteau Twins, The Cure, Depeche Mode, and Xmal Deutschland. And of course Killing Joke and Siouxsie—that went without saying. There were even short clips of movie dialog between each song, making for a singular experience.

A.J. knew he would have to up his game in the mix tape department.

They hit the theater with enough time to grab some good seats in the middle, and giggle at the stupid movie trivia slides before the show began. As expected, *Ghostbusters* was a hit, and both exited the cinema regarding the film as an instant classic. A.J. mused at the possibility of a group Halloween costume.

They briefly considered one of the restaurants near the Redwood for dinner, but ultimately decided on pizza and Skee-Ball at Gizmo's. So back into Lori's Datsun, more alternative rock at high volume as they headed back to Gold Beach, and an unbelievable parking spot directly in front of the arcade-restaurant with the green neon sign.

Gizmo's was hopping, and although A.J. recognized plenty of fellow students from Calico High, none of his gang made an appearance. He realized they were probably hanging out with Eren, planning to kick off the search the following morning.

They ate pizza slices and slurped soft drinks from waxed Coca-Cola cups, and during several rounds of Skee-Ball, Lori managed to elicit a wealth of background information from A.J.—about him, his friends, the town, and some heavily edited stories about their adventures a year ago.

In turn, A.J. found out that Lori's family had fled Vietnam when she was just two years old, and she'd been raised in a number of small towns up and down the California coast, wherever her folks could find work. With her dad landing a shift manager job at the cannery, Calico looked to be home, for a while anyway. Her mom's family had come to the States a couple years before them, and her uncle was making good money as a stock broker and financial planner in San Francisco. Lori's car, although used, had been a gift from him.

Full of pizza and high on infatuation, the two finally trundled out of Gizmo's with an armload of novelty prizes from the Skee-Ball ticket counter, and Lori took a slow and leisurely route back to A.J.'s house. Almost reluctantly, she pulled to a stop and shifted into neutral.

"I had fun," she sighed.

A.J. smiled. "Me too. We should do it ag—"

"What are you up to tomorrow?" Lori wondered, a bit too eagerly.

A.J. paused, clenching his jaw. "Oh, um...I'm supposed to go on a hike with the gang tomorrow." He immediately regretted making those plans, and the follow-up didn't help at all. "It's been in the works for a while now."

Lori refused to betray the slightest hint of disappointment. "No, it's totally cool. Just give me a call when you're free, and we'll do something."

She turned in her seat, brushing some hair from her eyes, and he nodded emphatically.

"Absolutely. It's a deal."

With the engine still idling, A.J. suddenly found Lori's face filling his view as she planted a soft kiss on his lips. Initially surprised, he relaxed and closed his eyes, inhaling the mixed scent of the car interior and what was either her bodywash or deodorant. Most of all, it was the Aqua Net. It was intoxicating, and he would forever associate the smell of that specific hairspray with his first proper kiss.

When she finally pulled back to look at him, her hands were clasped around his wrists, and a delicate finger probed the scar on his inside left arm. "What's this?" she asked, pulling the sleeve of his sweatshirt up so she could get a better look. A.J. panicked, yanking his arm away.

"It's nothing, just a..."

Lori's eyes blinked wide. "Is that a *brand?*" she grinned. "Kinky boy."

"No. Well, um, sort of," A.J. blushed, reaching for the passenger door handle. "Hey, I had a blast today. I'll...I'll call you."

An awkward yet electric moment passed between them, exhilarating and vulnerable all at once. Then he was gone, and she watched his retreat toward his house, shaking her head.

"Jesus, Lori," she muttered. "You sure love the weird ones, don't you?"

Track 16:
LOOKING FROM A HILLTOP

Section 25 (1984)

The Sunday morning streets of Calico were unsurprisingly clear of traffic, as most local residents either remained in bed or prepared to head to church. The Silver City Diner would open later in the morning to serve brunch to the after-worship crowd and late risers. The small town on the banks of the Rogue was stoically quiet, in stark contrast to the chaos and carnage of the past couple of days. Chaos and carnage generally kept locked away behind the scenes, unknown by the general populace, but present nonetheless.

The gang assembled at Liam's house at 8:30, with the sun already ascending in the eastern sky. Chlöe, Kris and Molly pulled up in the orange Corolla, and A.J. arrived solo on his bike. Day packs were stuffed with necessities for a long hike through the wilderness, with the knowledge that overnight camping would not be necessary, what with home being a quick teleport away.

There was no mysterious black sedan parked down the street from the Scott residence, unlike days previous. Although Eren maintained a general awareness of the local area, she felt a welcome sense of peace in place of the usual paranoia. Her only caution was to keep the volume down while talking to the others. Amber Scott was still sleeping inside, and the last thing she needed was an inquisitive mother asking questions.

Taking aim with a vaguely cylindrical electronic gadget adorned with various blinking lights and a small digital display screen, she burned a meter-wide glyph in the bed of the El Camino as the group collected in the carport.

"So you said you've never actually teleported from a moving car before..." Molly pondered, intrigued and more than a little worried.

Eren paused in thought. "Yeah, no," she admitted. "I've blinked to and from a ship—like the one you all rode in, but not from a moving ground vehicle." She watched most of the gathered friends swallow in unison, and tried to play off her admission with a simple hand wave. "It's theoretically possible, though." Noting their unchanged expressions, she added, "The principle is no different than traveling between static portals, or using your brand to jump to one."

"Since it's been a little while, maybe you should give us a refresher on the teleporting thing," A.J. suggested, and Eren nodded agreement.

"Good call," she said, shrugging out of her leather jacket to expose both of her toned, tan arms. The slightly raised scar of the teleport sigil was visible on the inside of her left forearm, just below the wrist. Identical to all the others, it resembled an equilateral triangle intersected by an invisible circle, which broke up the triangle's lines. At the center, a single point stood out, like a piece of lonely punctuation.

"The brand is a way to jump to a static portal. Like the one in A.J.'s room, or the one in the back yard here. Without a brand, anyone can travel between static gates by physically touching the sigils with bare skin—like you guys discovered back in Old Town Calico. That method can be a bit dangerous, because the exit location is any random gate unless you're recalling a portal you've been to."

"That's how we stumbled on the Black Eagle facility," A.J. remembered.

Molly offered a sarcastic laugh. "Lucky us."

Eren pursed her lips, facing the group with her arms at a downward angle, palms forward. "Correct. But a brand allows the traveler to jump to any static gate they've been to previously, from wherever they are at the moment, by completing a biometric circuit of sorts."

Crossing her right arm in front of her waist, she covered the scar on her left wrist with her hand, vanishing in a blinding flash of light. Ears popped as the local air pressure shifted to refill the void. Seconds later, she reappeared in the same manner, as if a powerful strobe had gone off in the bed of the El Camino.

Chlöe sighed, fascinated. None of them had teleported since Eren's departure the previous summer, and watching it was always a novel experience. "That. Is. Bad. Ass."

"Yeah," Liam pretended to yawn. "It's pretty cool."

"We won't be using the truck right away," Eren said, leaping gracefully from the back of the El Camino. "We may never need to. But everyone can use it if need be." Reaching into the bed, she hauled out her own day pack, pulling the straps over her arms. Even in the foothills of the Rogue River valley, it would be a warm day. She had layers in the form of flannel and microfiber, and a balled-up rain poncho, all stored within. A water canteen and assortment of Tiger's Milk protein bars and trail mix were the day's rations.

As Eren led the group into the back yard, she continued the briefing. "We're going to start at Hanging Rock, where I stowed the ship. Since I'm the only one who's been to that gate, you'll have to hang onto me this first time."

The group encircled her as she positioned herself in the center of the glyph burned into the mossy grass amidst random scraps of wood and concrete cinder blocks. She'd set the gate here over a year ago as a convenient waypoint between her special campsite up north, the various portals around Old Town, and the Black Eagle installation in the Siskiyou National Forest. The soil was ossified, glassy, refusing so much as a blade of new grass to emerge. Yet the surrounding vegetation was tall enough to obscure the shape from lateral view.

She squatted down, taking a knee within the intersected triangular sigil, each friend grasping her arms or shoulders with a bare hand. Eren touched two fingers to the center point of the sigil, and the world blinked away and reformed in an instant, with a rush of wind and flash of light. Suddenly their lungs were full of pine-scented air and the petrichor of trees and dew-covered grasses drying in the sun.

Hanging Rock overlook was a sheer granite cliff jutting proudly from the top of the trail, providing a commanding view of the surrounding forests and foothills, tinged with morning mist. A red-tailed hawk circled on a thermal current from the valley floor, searching for prey below.

Molly, Kris and Chlöe instantly vomited on the ground, A.J. wavering dizzily but keeping the contents of his stomach safely within.

Strangely, Liam showed no visible sign of disorientation or distress this time. "Rad," he muttered to himself, finally noticing the rest of the gang. "You guys okay?"

Eren squinted at her friend, reasoning out why he hadn't been affected by the jump. "Interesting," she said. "Could be all the cannabis you've been smoking this past year."

Liam just shrugged. "Sure. Let's say that."

Eren gestured toward the vista of Hanging Rock. "Well, we've got a lot of wilderness to cover. Ship's this way. Follow me."

As the group recovered with deep breaths and rinsing of mouths with canteen water, Molly trudged past Liam with a scowl. "I hate you."

Eren's ship stood a hundred yards distant, in a rocky depression just outside the edge of the forest. It looked identical to the vessel they'd liberated from the government facility in late 1982, saucer-shaped and ringed with rectangular viewports and a slightly raised center. It rested on a trio of landing struts, and had been covered in loose pine boughs in an attempt at rudimentary camouflage. Despite Hanging Rock being a popular hiking destination—and subject to even more traffic now that summer was here—Eren had taken care to park the vehicle away from any of the popular trails, such that locating it would require both knowledge to look for the craft and effort to get there.

She led the group into the gully, punching up a command on her cylindrical key. A mechanical release was followed by the quiet hydraulic whine of the entry gangplank lowering from the front of the ship.

Although their prior adventures had occurred on a different craft, there was still an overwhelming shared sense of exhilaration at boarding. It was hard not to grin stupidly as they entered the futuristic spacetime vehicle, with its molded synthetic control panels and cycling wireframe display screens.

Eren shrugged out of her pack and immediately began rifling through its contents, producing a folded map. Spreading it out on the center console, she pointed at several locations marked in red as the group gathered around.

"This point here was the origin of the distress signal to my Earth. There's a sigil there, and I've been to the area. They'd moved locations by the time I arrived, but it's a good starting place for the grid search."

Chlöe nodded at the map. "Lots of real estate to cover," she observed. "You wanna go in twos?"

"No way, Jose," Kris insisted. "Rule Number One."

In unison, the rest of the group—Eren included—chanted: "Never split up the party."

"We can spread out in the local area, but nobody goes off alone," Eren added. "Keep an eye out for anyone wearing the gray flight suit of the Black Eagles, like the one I was wearing when you first found me. If anything goes sideways, you can blink back to the Hanging Rock gate, or if you find one of the recovery team, bring them here to the ship." She gestured toward the floor to the right of the center console, where a purpose-built mechanical sigil glowed with soft blue light. "Barring that, you can always jump back to Liam's yard, or A.J.'s room, or the few gates in Old Town."

"Or the El Camino," Liam quipped.

Chlöe dismissed the details with a wave. "Yeah, yeah, we've got options."

"Point is, I don't want anyone getting hurt." Eren folded the map and replaced it in the pack, slinging it back over her shoulders and moving to the pulsating glyph in the ship's deck plate. "You guys ready? Huddle up."

Once again, the group circled around, reaching out touch her arms or back of her neck as she knelt in the center of the gate. Light exploded, air rushed in, and six friends vanished.

Track 17:
DIRTY CREATURE
Split Enz (1982)

The group appeared in a lightning flash, displacing a carpet of dry pine needles in a tiny shockwave. The clearing wasn't large, but held the party with a radius of ten feet to spare. It was ringed by old growth fir and ponderosa pine, hemlock and red alder. The big leaf maples were in full coverage, as were the dogwoods and ash. A waterfall tumbled down a moss-covered rocky incline in liquid tendrils, serenading the forest with its rush of white sound.

They fanned out, Kris and Molly pairing off together, Chlöe following suit.

Eren pointed toward the sigil scarred into the ground. "Everyone take a look around and commit this site to memory. If we need to, we can always rendezvous back here."

"How far out are we?" A.J. asked.

"Just over ten miles east of Hanging Rock," she answered, retrieving the map from her pack and opening it again for consultation.

"Wow," Chlöe said from the edge of the clearing. "You did some hiking. Nobody get lost."

Liam sighed. "Nobody *can* get lost. Not anymore. Just concentrate on one of the portals, and touch your brand. *Poof*—you're home."

"Oh. Yeah. Of course. I knew that."

Eren gestured into the forest. "We go east. That way."

As the group departed the clearing, spreading out into the thick woods, their chatter trailed away in the distance, eventually replaced by birdsong.

They hiked all day, through the ferns and deadfall, covering a six-mile grid around the original portal. Eren seared gate sigils into the forest floor in every grid center point, each a mile apart. Calling out repeatedly for the missing travelers, they heard nothing in reply but the singing of birds and timber creaking in the breeze. They found no trace of human activity, but did manage to surprise a doe with her young fawn. The deer leaped away into the bracken.

At last they called it good, with the sun low in the sky.

Knowing they were losing light, and it wasn't the best idea to go traipsing through the deep woods after dark, they reassembled at the first grid point in a burst of light, where the transmission had originated.

They were completely unaware of the cold eyes watching from behind a screen of brambles and wild blackberry vines.

There was still no sign that Eren's fugitives had been there in the interim, so they blinked back into Liam's yard. From there, the group dispersed to their various homes, and Eren and Liam went into the house to stow their packs and get some rest before the following day's search.

The night, unfortunately, had different plans.

Entering through the back door, they were struck by a pungent stench from deeper within the home. Liam flicked on some lights and ventured into the living room. His mom never worked Sunday nights, so she should have been around. Whether she was sober—or even conscious—was another matter completely.

"Mom?" he hailed. "You home?"

Eren wrinkled her nose in disgust. "Jesus, what is that smell?"

Liam sighed. There was a greater-than-zero chance that she was already passed out in bed, and might have fouled herself out of either end. "I'm gonna just check on her."

As his hand encircled the doorknob and cracked the bedroom door open, a part of him already knew something was wrong.

Very, very wrong.

Amber Scott lay on the unmade bed in an oversized t-shirt, her usual nighttime wear. The disheveled bedclothes and mattress were stained deep red, her normally tan complexion strangely pallid. The left side of her neck had been opened by what appeared to be a circular array of tiny knife points. She'd clearly been dead for some time.

Eren entered the room behind Liam and gasped in shock. On the floor beside the bed, next to the accumulated empty Jack Daniels and Wild Turkey bottles, lay an abomination she could never have imagined. Roughly six feet long, but seized in a rigid pose of obvious distress, its talon hands were curled in dramatic fashion, and its face and chin—very much the likeness of Liam's mother—were awash in crimson. Its lower body resembled that of a sleek furred animal, almost wolf-like, but with longer limbs and covered in some kind of viscous fatty substance. It almost appeared as if Amber Scott had put on a wet mink coat and just...melted in place.

The nausea Liam had held at bay throughout the day's portal jumping suddenly swelled in his throat, and he took a step back, into Eren's arms. "Holy shit."

"Oh god, Liam. What the hell—?" Eren clutched him in a firm embrace. Her supposed "cousin", adopted for appearances on the basis of ethnic similarity, had lost the only parent he knew. He was on his own in the world, and despite his being fairly self-sufficient, Eren knew from experience what a daunting prospect that was.

Of more immediate importance, what was this thing frozen in mid-transition on Amber Scott's bedroom floor? It was like something from a John Carpenter horror film, only real. And what was it doing here? Had her presence, with all of the teleportation activity, somehow drawn this creature here? If any of this was her fault, Eren decided, it was up to her to fix it.

"Holy shit," Liam repeated, spiraling into shock. "Shit. What the...what...the fuck."

Eren turned him, pulling him close. "I got you, Liam. I got you. Come on." She backed slowly from the bedroom, drawing him with her. "Just hang on, man. You gotta be strong for me, okay?"

Liam's eyes remained wide as saucers. "Eren, what...what *is* that?"

Holding him at arm's length, she met his eyes, regarding him with an almost military tone. "I need you to hold it together for a few minutes, okay? I want you to call Sheriff Chavez. I just need a minute in here."

Nodding, Liam shuffled to the mustard-yellow phone hanging on the kitchen wall, and dialed 9-1-1 for perhaps the first time since Oregon had implemented the program in 1981. He watched Eren disappear back into his mother's room and shut the door, then was barely aware of relating a torrent of information to the dispatcher. What he did remember, which would forever be carved into the granite of his long-term memory, were the words: *my mom is dead.*

℆

This was getting out of hand.

Chavez paced the living room of the small home, trying to fit the puzzle pieces together. There were no signs of struggle or forced entry to the home. Just two terrified kids, and one deceased single mom with a single wound on her neck and no blood in her body.

Lewis took notes as the EMTs bagged up Amber Scott's corpse, carting it away to Curry

General, where Dr. Bollinger would have another case to add to his files.

Liam leaned back in the rattan papa-san chair, gazing through Chavez with a thousand-yard stare. Eren sat attentively on the corner of the flower print sofa.

"So to recap," Chavez said, as much to herself as to the occupants of the room, "you two returned from hiking all day...where was it?"

"We were out around Hanging Rock," Eren explained. "Left about 9:30 this morning."

Lewis looked up from his notepad. "Was anyone else with you?"

"Sure," Eren said. "A.J., Kris, Molly, and Chlöe. We took one of the hiking trails out about six miles and back."

Lewis ran some mental numbers. "That's a long hike," he observed.

"And you got back at what time?" Chavez grilled.

Eren paused in thought. "About twenty, twenty-five minutes ago. Stowed our packs, came in and smelled that...horrible stench. Liam found his mom in her bed. Looked like she'd been there awhile."

The group fell silent as the medics wheeled the gurney out to the ambulance parked at the foot of the driveway.

Chavez nodded, taking it all in. "And when did you get back into town, Eren?"

"Late Thursday," she answered.

"I was out here Thursday night. I asked about you."

Liam blinked, joining the conversation out of thin air. "Yeah. She showed up about an hour after you told me mom was in jail for the night."

"Sheriff," Eren interjected. "What could have done that? To Amber, I mean. Some kind of animal?"

Chavez and Lewis both shuffled their feet in the rust-colored shag carpet.

"We've been getting reports of animal attacks in the area. That's all I can say right now. Investigation is ongoing." Chavez leveled a serious look at the two teens, softened with a motherly voice. "Do you feel safe in the house tonight?"

Eren and Liam consulted silently. "We can stay over at A.J.'s, or the Reynolds' tonight."

"Pack a bag," Chavez ordered. "And keep in touch."

Twenty minutes later, as Eren pulled the El Camino onto West Evergreen Drive, Liam silent in the passenger seat, she thought of the dead monstrosity duct-taped in a black tarp, hidden among the tall grass in the back yard. She hoped the cops didn't search too hard in the time it took to get to A.J.'s house. She could always blink back and retrieve the body, stash it in the forest, out from under the nose of law enforcement. Something told her having to explain the presence of a creature unknown to medical or zoological science wouldn't be the most effective way to complete her mission.

"We should have told her," Liam said aloud as they turned onto Hill Avenue, away from the river. "We need help. This is way above our pay grade."

Eren clenched her jaw. "I hear ya. But before we cross that bridge, we need to plan this out. Carefully."

They made the turn onto the ninety-degree bend of Ash Street, and as they rolled to a stop in front of the Jenkins house, Liam took note of three shimmering phantoms wandering near the trees at the end of the block. He pointed them out to Eren, who scowled.

"Shit. I was afraid of this."

A.J. came out as they exited the truck, his expression one of puzzlement. "What's up, guys?"

The revelation of Amber Scott's horrible death was a gut punch. Sure, she was largely absent from Liam's daily life, and there was always that pesky alcohol issue, but she'd been like a cool aunt to A.J. and Kris since junior high, when Liam had morphed from their tormentor to their protector. It had been Amber who got them in to see all those R-rated movies in years past—films which had been instrumental in A.J.'s creative and sexual awakening.

While A.J. went inside to phone Molly, inquiring about an emergency meeting and sleepover, Eren wandered off beyond the trees next to the house, vanishing in an explosion of light.

Liam and A.J. drove to the Reynolds house, informing the gathered friends of Liam's loss. There were tears and hugs, and Molly served up cans of soda to the bereaved.

"I'm so sorry, Liam," Chlöe whispered as she wrapped him in a gentle embrace.

"Dude, anything you need," Molly offered, eyes soft and glistening with tears. "Just ask."

Kris nodded agreement. "We're here for you, man."

Eren returned to the sigil burned into the vinyl flooring of the small basement kitchen, appearing in a blinding flash and burst of air.

"I blinked out to the first gate, stashed the creature there," she explained. "It's wrapped up pretty good, but I can't guarantee the local critters won't get to it. We need a plan, pronto."

A.J.'s childhood fascination with Sasquatch and other cryptids came raging to the forefront. "What was it? What do we know?"

The group settled in as Eren paced the basement floor. "I took a blood sample with the multi-key, so now I can scan for it, if we encounter a live one. Doesn't match anything in our records, but it did reveal a couple things. One, it had some of of Amber Scott's DNA. And two, it died of alcohol poisoning."

"So she was already wasted when it attacked her," Liam stated matter-of-factly. "That follows."

A.J. wasn't satisfied. "But what *was* it?"

"I've heard stories," Eren shrugged. "Other travelers from my world have encountered a species that fits the description. Animal intelligence. They can't create gates, but they can use existing portals. Their M.O. seems to be draining blood from the victim and then taking on its appearance, maybe as a way to camouflage or disguise long enough to escape."

Molly frowned in thought. "Like a mimic, from *D&D*..."

"Skin-walker," Liam muttered, and the room fell silent, all eyes on him. "Navajo legend, but a lot of tribes have similar stories.

Evil shape-shifting creature. Seems similar, anyway."

"I didn't think of that," Eren pondered. "But you're not wrong. It certainly has some of the hallmarks of the legends." She leaned against the pool table and folded her arms. "Possible that these things have been traveling ley lines and using natural nexus points to come and go. Might have been doing it for eons before we developed sigil technology to go point-to-point. But here's the real issue: if these things are using the portals I've been laying out, then all of this is my fault."

A.J. shook his head. "Eren, you had no way of knowing."

"Doesn't matter whether I knew or not," she replied. "I still have to take responsibility for it. If I hadn't been zapping gates all over the place, Liam's mom might still be alive."

"Irrelevant," Liam protested. "She was in the process of drinking herself to death." He glanced around the room at the sympathetic looks from his friends—his chosen family— and pressed on to clarify. "Whether it was booze or a monster from another dimension, she was heading for the exit."

"Dude..." Molly sighed. Her heart went out to him. After all, she and Bodhi still had *both* of their parents. It wasn't fair.

Kris spoke up: "So what do we do about it? You need the gates to get your team back."

"And I do want to get them back," Eren said. "But not at the expense of my friends and their community, which I dearly love. I've left portals all over the forest, and have no idea how many of those things have come through. I can't risk an infestation. For all our sakes, we need to get rid of them, with lethal force if necessary." She dropped her hands to brace them on the varnished walnut rim of the table.

"A.J., remind me how you closed the nexus point at the old mansion."

Track 18:
EVERYWHERE THAT
I'M NOT

Translator (1982)

On Monday morning, the Silver City Diner became the base of operations for a dual mission: closing Eren's teleportation gates while simultaneously searching for the recovery team survivors.

Shift workers scarfed down plates of eggs, bacon, and toast, while Deputy Lewis kept a watchful eye on the big booth packed with very animated teenagers. Eren had her map of the Siskiyou National Forest unfolded on the table, pointing at various areas marked in red.

"What y'all doing today?" Lewis inquired as he approached. "Another hike?"

A.J. smiled a little too broadly. "We're tracking wildlife for a summer project. Worth some extra credit in biology class next year." He winced internally—it sounded over-rehearsed.

Lewis was unconvinced. Locating Liam in the back of the booth, he offered a look of concern. "You okay to be out in the deep woods, son? Your mom died less than twenty-four hours ago."

Liam was sullen, and met the deputy's gaze with gravitas beyond his years. "Yeah, everyone keeps reminding me. I don't wanna think about it, Deputy. Honestly what I need is to get out of this friggin' town for awhile—get some fresh air and be with the family I have left."

"Fair enough," Lewis admitted, relaxing his stance a bit. "Seems like you're in good hands." Backing away from the table, he added, "You be careful out there. Don't wanna have to send a search and rescue team out for ya."

"You don't have to worry, Deputy," Eren assured him. "We're all experienced hikers."

Lewis nodded. "Okay then. As you were. Have fun."

Eren kept Lewis in her line of sight as he exited the diner, noting that although he got into his vehicle, it did not move from its parking spot. "How we doing on work schedules?" she asked.

"I went in to talk to Gary at the garage this morning," Liam reported, more to the group than to Eren, who had been with him. "Taking a couple weeks off to bury my mom."

Kris cast a furrowed glance at his friend. Every time someone mentioned Amber's death, it was another emotional body blow. "I got the week off," he said.

"Me too," A.J. added, also noticing the Bronco's lack of movement outside. He leaned forward conspiratorially. "I still say we should tell him. We should clue in Chavez. At least with them in the loop, we won't be the ones getting in trouble."

"In trouble?" Liam scoffed. "Dude, we're dealing with interdimensional shape-shifting parasites, and a secret government agency who murdered a sheriff's deputy and made it look like a suicide. Local law enforcement is the least of our worries."

A.J. stood from the booth seat, frowning. "That's precisely my point."

Suddenly an arm hooked around him, and Lori directed him away from the table, smiling. "Just borrowing A.J. for a moment. He'll be right back."

The group watched in amazed silence as she pulled A.J. over toward the alcove that served as the arcade. The corners of Eren's mouth crept upward as she observed the interaction.

"Sorry to interrupt your top secret meeting," Lori began. "I actually wanted to apologize for that kiss Saturday night after our date. You clearly weren't ready—"

This time it was A.J.'s turn to act completely on impulse. Cradling Lori's head in his hands, he leaned in, passionately meeting her lips with his. Their tongues gently probed back and forth in an awkward dance, and A.J. once again became lost in the scent of cloves and Aqua Net.

The moment seemed to last forever, as all eyes in the booth got wider and wider, A.J.'s friends observing something that they never dreamed would happen. Certainly not pushing sixteen, and maybe not ever.

Finally he pulled away, his hands still framing her face. Her expression was one of simultaneous shock and giddiness.

"I-I uh..." Lori stammered. "Wow."

"I was *so* ready," A.J. assured her. "I was just scared to drag you into this...stuff we have going on."

"Well let's start there," she suggested, wiping a smear of black lipstick from his lower lip with her thumb. "You like me. I like you."

"Agreed."

"You want to spend time with me?"

"Yes."

"Good, 'cause I want to spend time with you," she smiled. "So let me into your little club, and we can kill birds with stones in the bush, or whatever."

A.J. cringed like a child being made to wear a scratchy wool sweater for a Sears holiday portrait. There were two distinct issues here: Lori's safety and Eren's true mission. "I...would love to, seriously. But...I don't want to put you in any danger..."

"Dude," Lori chided. "My parents fled a war zone with a two-year-old baby. Growing up weird and Asian in America? I laugh in the face of danger. I give noogies to the very notion of fear."

A.J. managed a weak smile. "I don't doubt you could give death a purple nurple."

"Damn straight," Lori replied with a look so full of confidence that A.J. felt himself stepping over the precipice.

"Just...give me a few days. Let me take care of this immediate thing. Okay?"

"I dunno," Lori shook her head in faux hesitation. "I've got dudes all over Curry County lining up to date me."

Holding her shoulders, he leaned in to plant another kiss on her forehead. "I'll take 'em all on."

Lori sighed, dejected, and A.J. offered a wistful smile. As he rejoined the group at the table, Eren scooted out and whispered something to Lori on her way to the restroom, and she followed.

"So," A.J. said casually as he slid onto the seat, "do we have a plan for the sea salt and vinegar solution?"

The group stared blankly back at him.

"What was that?" Molly grinned.

Liam chuckled, offering a mug of coffee in salute. "Way to go, stud muffin."

"That's *Mister* Stud Muffin," Chlöe corrected with a twinkle in her blue eyes.

A.J. grunted an exasperated sigh. "*Doctor* Stud Muffin, thank you very much. I didn't spend four post-graduate years at Stud Muffin University for nothing."

"Um, if we can give A.J.'s love life a rest for a minute," Kris interjected, "I've got the supplies handled. We can mix up a big batch when we're done here."

Liam took a sip from his coffee cup. "We can use my sprayer, like we did before."

"My dad has one too," A.J. added. "Just in case we need to split up."

"I thought that Rule Number One was never split up the party," Chlöe said.

Molly shrugged. "Yeah, well, sometimes you gotta break the rules."

"There are gates all over the area," A.J. explained. "Each of our houses. Three at Old Town alone. The one by the pond where Eren ditched her first ship. The camping spot up near Rock Creek. The one out at Hanging Rock. Six, no...*seven* in the forest. Not to mention the one in the bed of Liam's truck. No wonder we've been seeing phantoms without needing a delicious pumpkin cookie." He glanced over at Kris, who threw up his hands.

"Dude, they're seasonal. I don't make the rules."

"In any case," A.J. continued, "It's gonna take some time and effort to close 'em all down."

Chlöe nodded. "Before any more of those...creatures come through."

"Yeah," Liam warned. "You don't want any part of that."

As the last of the planning finished up, Eren and Lori appeared from the restroom and approached the table.

"Shall we get started?" Eren asked.

In the midst of the general affirmative murmur, A.J. noticed that Lori was flexing her left hand into a fist.

Taking her aside, he fixed her with a look of concern. "You okay? What's up?"

"Eren and I had a good talk," she explained. "Really productive."

Then she pulled the left sleeve of her cardigan to her elbow, revealing the familiar scar of a teleportation sigil branded into the flesh of her arm.

"Guess I'm going with you guys."

Track 19:
COLLAPSING NEW PEOPLE
Fad Gadget (1984)

On the night of October 29th, 1982, a group of five friends had closed a ley line nexus located in the ballroom of the abandoned McCabe mansion at the top of Timber Hill Road, as a seemingly endless parade of phantoms from some dead dimension streamed out of it.

They'd used a recipe of sea salt and white vinegar, and delivered it in the form of squirt guns and water balloons, and a canister used for spraying weeds. Perhaps most impressively, they'd completed the task while fending off the attention of bullies, avoiding law enforcement, and wearing Halloween costumes.

Now they had to do it half a dozen times over. Fortunately without the costumes, but now with federal agents dogging their every move, and the local sheriff not too far off the scent. Oh yeah, and some pesky dimension-hopping monsters who drained your blood and assumed your appearance. That was a fun new wrinkle.

An hour after leaving the diner, seven friends stood outside Liam's house on West Evergreen. The group had expanded in the almost two years since the Great Haunted Mansion Nexus Closure of '82. They'd befriended a traveler from another dimension, broken into a secret government installation, stolen a spaceship (though Molly preferred the term "liberated"), fought off legions of alien drones (in space), and lived to tell the tale...metaphorically-speaking. They couldn't *actually* tell the tale to anyone outside the group. A group which now included said dimensional traveler, and the newest addition, Lori Tran.

It was a done deal. Whatever happened between Lori and A.J. in the future, she was a part of this now. In the span of five minutes in the diner bathroom, Eren had told her everything, and she hadn't batted an eye. Hearing about the gang's previous adventures had only deepened Lori's interest in A.J., and her unflinching belief and fearlessness had done the same for him.

They were dressed for the woods, in jeans and hiking boots, hoodies and windbreakers. Lori had shed the plaid miniskirt in favor of black Levi's. Liam had his old olive drab Army jacket draped over the side of the El Camino's bed, which also contained two spray canisters and an assortment of water pistols full of the Old World recipe, courtesy of Grandma Korolewski.

Their strategy was simple: teleport to the first portal, douse it with the vinegar solution, then travel to the next. They'd work backward from the grid points in the forest, leaving the sigil at Hanging Rock for a quick getaway.

Eren *hoped* the sigils would be disabled with the liquid, anyway. She'd never actually *closed* a gate before. Hearing that the gang had managed to shut down a massive nexus point with the stuff had been a revelation. To be fair, it was a pretty "woo-woo" contrivance proffered in new age bookstores next to the quartz crystals and books on astral projection. No one had ever heard of such a thing in her world. Perhaps chemistry worked differently here. Or differently *enough*.

Liam would drive the El Camino out to a remote area off Silver Creek Road, to one of the old logging spurs, where he would park in the off chance they needed to teleport out with some easy mobility at hand. He would have one of the two spray canisters in the truck. Kris would wear the second one on his back.

"Everyone take a water pistol," Eren ordered as Liam passed out translucent squirt guns in various vibrant colors.

"They're more .for personal protection," Liam said, "in case the phantoms get frisky."

Kris laughed. "Wasn't that a Saturday morning cartoon? *Frisky Phantom*?"

"*Funky Phantom*," Molly scoffed. "Dumbass."

Kris rolled with the insult. "It's pronounced *doo-MAH*. It's French." To which Molly replied with a middle finger. Kris feigned shock, gasping and clutching at imaginary pearls. "I'm telling Bodhi!"

Eren sighed, coming to grips with the fact that when it came to top secret interdimensional operations, beggars simply could not be choosers. She stepped to the center of the driveway and was about to address the group when she noticed Liam zipping up his backpack, a bottle of Wild Turkey bourbon cradled within.

"Hey," she said quietly, gripping his arm, "you don't need to follow your mother's path."

Liam locked eyes with his transdimensional cousin. "And *you* don't need to worry about that. It's just a backup." Her expression was quizzical as he set the pack in the bed of the truck, opened the driver's side door, and fished the keys from his front pocket. "Who's coming with me up Silver Creek Road?"

"I'll go with you," Chlöe answered, moving to the passenger side of the truck.

In truth, Chlöe's heart had been breaking on Liam's behalf. She couldn't imagine being alone at sixteen, and felt a certain nascent maternal instinct developing in his general direction.

The El Camino rumbled to life, and Liam waved at his friends as he and Chlöe drove away.

"Everyone else," Eren said, "follow me to the back yard."

She gathered them in a semicircle, pointing toward the teleportation sigil in the tall grass. "This is mostly for Lori's benefit. Take a mental picture of this location in case you need to travel here."

A.J. traded a look with Lori. "You got it?"

"I got it," she affirmed.

"It's gonna feel really weird the first time."

Eren nodded. "He's not wrong. It takes some getting used to." Taking a knee in the center of the glyph, she added, "Okay, everyone on me. Going to close the first gate."

Once again, all hands clutched her arms and the back of her neck. A.J. snaked an arm around Lori's slender waist, and she pressed into him. In a flash of light, they were gone.

Lori felt her ears pop as the scenery shifted from Liam's back yard to the deep woods of the Siskiyou National Forest. The crisp grass underfoot became moss and evergreen needles, and the breeze from the river was replaced with a still, pine-scented heat. Luckily, she'd eaten a light breakfast. Unfortunately, what there was beat a hasty retreat from her stomach. She turned, retching on the forest floor.

A.J. maintained his hold on her hips, supporting her body as she emptied everything onto the ground. "Don't worry," he assured her. "It gets easier."

Liam was unaffected, as before. Kris and Molly seemed less nauseous than the last time. A.J. was too focused on steadying Lori to be sick.

"Everyone okay?" Eren asked, taking a visual survey of the clearing. "Kris, you good to go?"

Nodding stoically, Kris stepped forward, unslinging the canister from his back, and pumping the handle on top to pressurize the contents. "On it," he said as he aimed the spray wand toward the sigil on the ground, letting loose a stream of clear solution.

While Kris worked, Eren went to the underbrush nearby and verified that the dead creature wrapped in plastic was still there, unmolested by predators.

"I think I'm done," Kris announced. All eyes focused on the gate, expecting some sort of visual cue that it was no longer functional. All that occurred was a quiet sizzling sound and bit of evaporating mist, like a drop of water on a hot skillet.

"Huh," Molly grunted. "Is that it?"

Eren pointed the electronic key at the shape burned into the forest floor, and observed the digital reading. "Non-functional," she said. "It worked. Let's move on."

Once again, they huddled up on Eren, and once more Lori felt her insides rebel. A.J. was right, however. It wasn't as bad this time. It was a little like the first time she'd taken a bong hit.

The second portal was sealed in the same manner, with Kris hosing down the sigil and Eren confirming it was properly disabled. By the third gate, Lori was getting the hang of the teleportation thing, and barely burped as they appeared deeper in the forest, surrounded by more old growth trees than she'd ever seen in one place. A.J. handed her a roll of Wint-O-Green Life Savers, which she readily accepted.

"Okay guys," Eren said. "Halfway there. Let's go."

The fourth portal was in a clearing on an incline, with a fern-covered sweep toward the base of the foothill. They heard the flies almost before they arrived in the usual burst of light and displaced air. Fleshy remnants of some large animal were strewn haphazardly near the roots of a Douglas fir. Except it wasn't just any animal—it was human.

Lori gagged, and it wasn't due to the jump.

"What is that?" Molly wondered aloud.

A.J. felt an electric charge down his spine as he pointed toward the person emerging from the trees.

Eren followed his gesture, eyes growing wide. "Risha?"

"Is that one of your people?" Kris asked.

The woman was slender, like Eren. She looked no older than twenty, dark complected and dressed in shreds of the familiar gray flight suit Eren had first appeared in. She didn't speak, but appeared shell-shocked, traumatized, and moved toward the assembled teens with open arms.

Eren raised the multi-key and consulted the scanner. "Heads up," she warned. "It's not her!" She glanced down and realized that the pile of body parts at her feet was in fact Risha, not the person before them.

The group fell silent as the thing with Risha's face began to change. Its body seemed to convulse as the outward facade of human appearance was absorbed into a sinewy, glistening form of alien appendages and an almost insectoid face. Multiple sets of glossy black eyes surrounded a pulsating maw filled with hundreds of needle-thin teeth. Bony talon digits sprouted from elongated arms, flexing and spreading...flexing and spreading.

It growled hungrily, and lunged.

Everyone ducked as gunfire erupted from the tree line behind them, ripping through the creature, rending the alien torso into pieces. The main portion of the thing dropped at Eren's feet, spasmed momentarily, and fell still.

She turned to see Sheriff Chavez and Deputy Lewis step from the brush, shotguns in hand. There was a prolonged, awkward silence before anyone spoke.

Kris swallowed. "How did you—?"

"Find you?" Lewis finished. "That lab facility Halverson was surveilling is about a quarter mile east of here. Lots of activity in the deep woods today, and sound can really travel. You're not exactly being quiet."

"Failed stealth roll," Kris sighed with a pout.

Molly slapped his shoulder. "Dude, no."

"I assume," Chavez began, "that you're gonna tell me what the hell that thing was?" She looked the group of teens over, noting Kris with the weed sprayer canister slung on his back.

Eren sighed. "Yes. I will. Promise."

"Right now."

A.J. raised a hand. "It's just that we have to—"

"I wasn't asking."

Lewis popped a couple fresh shells into the side of the Remington. "Does this thing have any connection to Amber Scott's murder?"

Eren responded with a blank look. How had Lewis connected those dots?

"I saw you blink out of Liam's back yard last night," the deputy explained. "Pretty neat trick."

Chavez squinted at Eren. "And about that..."

A.J. came to Eren's defense with an abridged explanation he hoped would work. "Eren is from an alternate Earth. They've figured out how to teleport through special gates. She's trying to find some of her people who escaped federal custody. And these creatures use the same gates to travel."

More stunned silence. Chavez and Lewis exchanged a look, and she finally nodded. "That follows."

A.J.'s jaw dropped. "It does?"

"More than you know," Chavez shook her head, bemused. "But when this is over, you, your friends and I are gonna have a long talk."

At that moment, a squad of ten federal agents in dark suits and aviator shades emerged from the opposite end of the clearing, automatic rifles aimed squarely at the group.

"FEDERAL AGENTS! DROP YOUR WEAPONS AND GET ON THE GROUND, NOW!"

Kris and Molly winced in unison. Chavez and Lewis began silently reviewing tactics in their heads. A.J. and Lori traded a look of apprehension, and Eren's shoulders fell.

"God *damn* it."

Track 20:
UNDER THE GUN
Circle Jerks (1983)

The agents were armed with M-16s, had the high ground, and were numerous enough to cover everyone within the clearing.

Chavez and Lewis raised their hands. "Curry County Sheriff's Department," Chavez hailed, still gripping the shotgun. "The kids are unarmed."

"DROP THE GUNS AND GET ON YOUR KNEES," came the order from the tree line, and Chavez nodded at Lewis.

"Do it," she ordered, motioning toward the group of teens. "You too."

In unison, Lewis and Chavez lowered their respective weapons to the ground, moving slowly and calmly.

Suddenly and without warning, the feds cried out in terror as they were savaged by alien claws and teeth from the trees behind them. Agents vanished, hauled backward into the dense brush. Gunfire and screams echoed into the woods as Eren's group scattered from the clearing. Chavez and Lewis snatched their shotguns from the ground and followed close behind.

Running blind as the trees and vegetation rushed past, the gang headed as quickly as possible toward any serviceable hiding spot.

Eren caught Kris pausing behind the massive stump of an old fir tree. Molly crouched nearby. "Lose the canister," Eren ordered, and he shrugged it loose, dropping it at her feet. Eren slung the strap over one arm. "Jump to the truck. Go now."

Kris was confused. "Truck? I don't understand..."

"Don't argue, Kris. We don't have time. Shit is on fire and I need you safely out of here."

She gestured at Molly. "Jump to the truck. Now."

The two traded uncertain looks, then touched their brands in unison. Two slightly offset flashes pierced the sultry summer gloom of the deep woods, and they were gone. More agonized cries in the distance were punctuated by the erratic *pop-pop-pop* of automatic fire.

Eren scanned the wilderness around her. "Fucking hell," she huffed, setting out east at a quick jog.

⁜

"Looks like we finally crossed the line with the feds," Lewis quipped, dodging through a copse of alders as gunfire rang out through the trees.

"Crossed the line?" Chavez answered with a sarcastic chuckle. "Deputy Lewis, we crossed that line when Halverson figured out what they were up to. I'm not about to let them win this fight."

"We've got shotguns and sidearms," Lewis protested. "They've got numbers, and military hardware. What's wrong with this picture?"

He wasn't joking. They were seriously out-gunned and outnumbered. And although he was thankful for the distraction provided, he'd seen enough horror films to know that the shape-changing alien monster was never the good guy. There was also no way of knowing how many of those things were currently prowling the forest, or where.

The feds seemed to have been between the predators and their little group by sheer luck of the draw. With everyone scattered, it was anyone's guess where any particular agent or creature might pop up.

"Sheriff, over here!"

It was A.J., beckoning over a giant fallen tree to their right.

Chavez skirted the end of the log, and Lewis went over the top, landing in the soft carpet of moss, shotgun in hand. A.J. and Lori looked more determined than frightened, and Chavez considered that somewhat unsettling. No kid should have to witness what just happened in the clearing back there. The fact that they weren't curled in a fetal position in absolute shock spoke well of their mental fortitude, but not so well of the state of the world.

"Sheriff, I'm gonna let you guys in on something," A.J. said with more gravity than any fifteen-year-old she'd ever known. "But you gotta trust me."

Lori backed away from the group, apprehension written on her face. "I'll go ahead. Meet you at the truck."

A.J. reached out reactively. "Lori, wait!"

Closing her eyes, she envisioned the bed of the El Camino, and the sigil etched into it. Her finger grazed the scar on the inside of her wrist, and she vanished in light.

Chavez and Lewis blinked, looked at each other, then back at the empty space Lori had occupied only moments earlier.

"That is just the damnedest thing," Lewis stammered, shaking his head in disbelief.

A.J. locked eyes with Chavez. "I can get us out of here," he promised. "Please. You have to trust me."

Finally Chavez nodded.

"Hold onto me," he instructed, and each grasped a shoulder with their free hand. A.J. brushed his index finger across the brand on his arm, imagining the El Camino.

Lightning flashed in the forest, and the three were gone.

☙

The black sedan had been tailing Liam since Myrtle Tree Bridge. He'd never had a chance to find a hiding place off the rural highway, and they were making no attempt to disguise their motives—they were on his ass. And when you had the feds on your ass, you truly *had* someone on your ass.

His original plan had been to head out to Silver Creek Road, and the multitude of fire trails and logging spurs that branched from it. But when Chlöe noted the black Ford, Liam made an executive decision to continue on Jerry's Flat, the larger of the river frontage roads. Following the curve of the Rogue, Jerry's Flat became Agness at Lobster Creek Road, continuing to the southeast. This route would allow Liam to take advantage of faster speeds and more maneuvering room.

When Molly and Kris appeared in the back of the truck, Liam did a double-take. His rear view mirror was instantly blocked with bodies, disoriented and traveling at fifty miles-per-hour. The sudden shift in cargo weight made the El Camino pull to the right, and Liam down-shifted, compensating with the wheel to recover.

Despite Eren saying they should test the theory, they'd never had the chance. Now it had been proved. You *could* teleport to a moving ground vehicle. Not that it wasn't hell on the suspension.

There was a general murmur of confusion from the back as the two reoriented, squatting down into safer positions. Kris pressed his back into the second spray canister in the front corner of the bed. Liam pointed a thumb out the driver's side window, and the three realized they were being followed.

There was another flash, and another. Lori appeared in the center of the gate and immediately toppled forward into Molly's lap. Then

A.J. and Curry County's finest arrived with a *whoosh* of displaced air.

When A.J. had decided to send four people into the back of the El Camino, he didn't know it was already carrying Kris and Molly. The truck became instantly heavier as it rumbled down the road, fishtailing with the added weight.

Lewis looked nauseous, and Chavez let loose a stream of vomit over the side. A.J. lost his balance and launched backward over the wheel well, landing in a massive collection of ferns and scotch broom on the roadside. Lori cried out after him, watching the black sedan pull up close by. But before the agents could get out of the car to detain him, he was gone again in a flash of light. The feds were only temporarily confused, clambering back into their vehicle and resuming the chase as A.J. reappeared in the truck bed.

Within moments, they'd closed the gap, pulling nearer to the rear of the speeding El Camino.

Fifty miles-per-hour. Fifty-five. Sixty. Trees and rural power poles zipped by in a blur.

An agent in sunglasses leaned out the passenger window of the sedan, taking aim with a pistol.

A.J. found Lori in the front of the truck bed. She looked paler than usual.

"First solo jump," he grinned. "Good job."

She managed a weak smile in response, and he gently took her hand. "Got one more in you?"

As Chavez and Lewis watched, Lori nodded. "Sure. Where to?"

"Hold onto me," he said, kneeling in the center of the gate. With Lori's arms hugging him around his neck and shoulders, he laid his hand on the sigil and vanished.

The sudden reduction in weight caused the El Camino to surge forward, Liam wrestling back control as the agent behind them fired, his shot going wide.

There was another blinding flash, and an unholy shape-shifter from the forest lunged forward from the sigil. Kris and Molly froze in abject horror as the creature's talons clutched in front of its oily, sinewy torso, mouth full of needle teeth probing the air toward them.

Its bite found Chavez's shoulder, and she screamed in agony, ripping herself away instinctively but rending the flesh and muscle from the multitude of barbs as she did so. Her left arm went numb almost instantly, and her shotgun clattered to the metal bed.

Kris kicked at the beast, creating enough space for Lewis to get his gun under the thing's hideous head and fire. The shot ruptured out the back of its upper portion, sending blood and viscera across the windshield of the sedan. Lewis racked another shell into the chamber and fired a second time, blasting a hole through its chest.

It staggered momentarily, rocking back and forth.

Grasping around for anything vaguely weapon-like, Molly reached into Liam's pack next to the spray canister, drawing the bottle of Wild Turkey out by its neck like a Whack-a-Mole paddle. Swinging with both hands, she brought the heavy container across ithe creature's head, glass and bourbon exploding from the impact. The predator screamed in agony as alcohol splashed across its upper body.

Yet it still stood its ground, swaying in a daze with the motion of the truck.

Molly was struck by sudden inspiration. Launching herself forward, she hit the creature like a linebacker, squarely where the ribcage would have been on a human being. Her momentum sent both of them sailing over the tailgate. The creature impacted the hood of the Ford, crushing the intake manifold.

Veering hard to the left, the sedan flipped side-over-side, pieces of metal and fiberglass rocketing in all directions as it finally came to rest on the wooded roadside, a shattered mess. One wheel sheared loose and bounced along the road, passing the El Camino as Liam slowed, wrestling with the wheel.

Kris barely had time to form Molly's name in his mouth before there was another flash of light, and she sprawled on the sigil. He immediately gathered her into his arms. "Jesus. You scared the crap outta me."

Her breath came fast and heavy. "Holy shit, that was close."

☙

A.J. and Lori appeared inside the sigil at Hanging Rock, crouched like wrestlers sizing up an opponent, but there were no others in the vicinity. The air was still, sun warm on their faces. From miles away, the occasional *pop* of gunfire could still be heard echoing across the wilderness.

"Come on," A.J. urged, moving toward the small canyon to the north. "Eren's ship is over here."

Lori swayed dizzily as she took a step. "Why didn't you just jump there?" she demanded, stopping to catch her bearings.

A.J. looked back. "I dunno. I just visualized this gate. Spur of the moment."

"Hold it right there," a voice hailed from a clump of rhododendron trees to their left.

Lori and A.J. froze in place as a man stepped from the vegetation, some kind of futuristic-looking weapon leveled in their direction. He appeared to be in his early twenties, tall, tan and ethnically Native American. His dark hair was shaved on the sides, pulled back from his face in a small topknot. Most notably, he wore the gray flight suit of the Black Eagle squadron. "You used the gate," the man said. "Who are you?"

A.J. was about to answer when a blast of light erupted behind them, and Eren stepped off the sigil on the ground.

"A.J.! Lori!" she cried, approaching from behind. She slowed as she noticed the man emerging from the bushes. "Marc?"

"Eren?" said the man, lowering the weapon in front of him.

Producing the multi-key from her pocket, she took a quick reading, smiling as she noted the results. "It's him."

"Who's *him*?" Lori wondered.

"Marc," was Eren's only answer as she dropped the canister and rushed to the man's embrace.

Track 21:

TRUST ME

Mick Karn (1982)

Liam slowed to a stop at the next turnout, and Chlöe leaped from the passenger seat to check on the riders in the back. Deputy Lewis held Sheriff Chavez in a pair of broad arms as she kept pressure on her wound. The gash in her collar bone was deep, and the left side of her uniform shirt was dark with blood. Her arm hung limply at her side.

Kris and Molly were tangled together at the front of the truck bed behind the rear window. Both looked traumatized.

Reaching behind the driver's seat, Liam produced a first aid kit in an aluminum case. He handed it across the bed to Chlöe, who had already climbed up and was tending to Chavez.

"What the hell happened?" Liam demanded.

Kris leaned over, his grip on Molly unwavering. "We got the first four sigils," he sighed. "But then we found the remains of someone Eren called *Risha*. And one of those creatures. And these two found us, and killed the thing. But then the feds popped up out of nowhere. And more of those creatures attacked. And here we are."

"Not out of nowhere," Lewis interjected.

Liam frowned. "What?"

Lewis propped Chavez against the cab window as Chlöe broke open the first aid kit and went to work. "Deputy Halverson was looking into Project Black Eagle. In fact, it's what got him killed. There's a secret facility not far from where those agents showed up."

"Yeah," Liam grunted, shrugging. "We've been there." His shoulders and neck were on fire, and he realized just how tense he'd been throughout the chase.

Lewis blinked in disbelief. "You've been—"

"But Eren said that place was mothballed." Liam glanced down for validation from Kris and Molly. Both nodded.

"Yeah, well the old tenants have moved back in." Lewis stood in the truck bed, stretching his limbs and hoisting the shotgun to reload. "These shapes," he said, nodding at the sigil burned into the back of the truck, "you use them to...to teleport?"

"Yeah," Liam affirmed. "Sort of. They're waypoints. You can use them without a brand to go from gate to gate. With a brand, you can go from anywhere to any gate."

Lewis pointed a finger at Kris. "I saw you spraying the one in the forest with a canister like that one." He indicated the second weed sprayer behind the cab. "What's up with that?"

Kris stared straight ahead, arms tight around Molly's shoulders. "It's vinegar and sea salt. It closes the portal. Makes it non-functional."

Lewis let his look of abject bewilderment last about two seconds before he decided to move on. "Well if those things can use the...what did you call it? A gate?" He regarded Liam with a discerning look. "Why don't you hose this one down?"

"Because some of our group is still out there," Liam explained. "And they may need to get to us quickly."

"Yeah?" Lewis retorted. "Well so can those critters."

"Relax," Liam assured the deputy, without any good reason for his confidence. "You've got some firepower."

Chlöe applied a large gauze pad to the wound on the sheriff's neck and shoulder, wrapping it tightly with a roll of the same material. "We need to get her to the hospital," she advised.

"No," Chavez protested. "Take me to my office."

Chlöe squinted, confused. "Ma'am?"

"We're not safe out here, as long as these agents are prowling around. And those monsters."

"No shit," Molly agreed, beginning to surface from her state of shock.

Lewis pumped a shell into the chamber and nodded. "She's right. We need backup. We need to be on our home turf." He looked Liam squarely in the eyes. "And we need some answers from you kids."

Liam sighed. He couldn't argue with the basic facts. They were vulnerable out here, away from what passed for civilization in rural Oregon. "Fair enough," he said, gesturing at Kris and Molly. "Kris, you've got a license. You guys jump back to Molly's place, take the family wagon and get out to the Sheriff's Department in Gold Beach. We'll meet up there."

"Got it," Kris acknowledged. He wasn't wild about teleporting again, but he knew it had to be done. Still holding Molly close, he leaned his face to her head and reached across to touch the scar on his arm. They vanished in a blinding flash, and Lewis swallowed to pop his ears.

"Yeah," he muttered aloud. "Lots of answers."

Liam caught Chlöe's gaze across the back of the truck. "Is she stable?"

"For now," Chlöe said with a brief shrug.

"Okay, let's get her in the front, with me," Liam instructed. "The ride will be easier on her."

Within a couple of minutes, Chavez was strapped in the passenger seat, Chlöe and Lewis in the back. Liam revved the El Camino and steered onto the rural highway, back in the direction of Gold Beach.

Lewis grabbed the sheriff's shotgun and handed it to Chlöe. "You ever shoot one of these?"

Chlöe swallowed her trepidation and tried to put on a brave face. "Of course," she assured him, resting the gun across her legs.

The trip would take the better part of an hour, with the constant threat of vampiric creatures teleporting onto the sigil in the bed of the truck. It happened twice more, within minutes of departure. Lewis and Chlöe simultaneously blasted the first one as it appeared, Lewis booting it in the center of mass, sending it over the tailgate and tumbling into the road. Chlöe blasted the second one under its head, a fountain of bloody viscera streaming into the air behind them. Angling the shoulder stock in her right hand, she swept to the left, bashing it sideways over the wheel well, into the brush.

The steering went squirrelly with the sudden changes in cargo weight, but with some concentration and effort, Liam kept control of the truck.

In the passenger seat, Chavez flexed her hand in to a fist. The feeling was returning to her arm, although the immediate area around the wound was still thankfully numb. "You held out on me, kid." Her words dripped with disappointment.

"I know," Liam replied, hands gripping the wheel.

"I always had your back."

"I know."

Several quiet moments passed, then Chavez asked, "How long?"

Liam took a deep breath. "We discovered the gates around Old Town during the summer two years ago, when Eric Somerville and Jeannie Wells went missing. Then Eren showed up that December. We helped her get her ship out of the facility, and deliver a weapon that saved her Earth from an alien invasion." He paused, adding, "Sounds crazy, I know."

"Do you?" Chavez demanded. "Do you really? *¡Dios mío!* What a clusterfuck."

Liam continued driving, eyes glued to the road. "...Yeah."

❧

A.J. and Lori watched as Eren gripped the stranger in a tight hug.

"Holy shit, Marc, I'm so glad you made it."

The man reciprocated her embrace, then stepped back at arm's length to look at her. "Eren...how the hell did you...there's just so much to tell."

"We got your distress call," Eren explained. "I'm not sure how you cobbled together the tech to send it, but I'm glad you did." She suddenly remembered the two teens standing by, observing the reunion. "These are my friends. A.J. and Lori."

Marc stepped forward, extending a hand, and A.J. shook it.

"Local assets, reporting for duty."

The man laughed. "Good to meet you, 'local assets'. Any friends of my baby sister are friends of mine."

A.J. exchanged a knowing look with Lori. "That explains the family resemblance." He hefted the spray canister by the strap, slinging it over one shoulder.

"Is it just you?" Eren asked. "Where's the rest of the team?"

Marc exhaled, shoulders sagging. "Zahna died during our escape. We got back to the mothballed facility in the forest and scavenged enough components to send our message back, but without a multi-key, we had limited travel options. Federal agents and military kept closing in, and we ended up getting separated. I spent a long time going back and forth between the federal facility and that old mine near the town on the river, using the existing gates."

"Old Town Calico," A.J. offered. "We found your sigils. The mine, the livery stable, the turnout. Learned how to use them the hard way."

Marc looked A.J. over, noting the scar on his left arm. "You're branded."

"I did it," Eren admitted. "A.J. and his friends helped me deliver the weapon. They're heroes."

"You...you delivered the weapon?" Marc breathed, eyes wide in amazement. "So it...it worked?"

Eren winked at A.J. as if to say, *you take this one.*

"It worked," A.J. nodded. "We helped Eren break the ship out. My friends manned the weapon systems, and I fired the big one. With the invaders' mother ship out of the game, the drones just...shut down." He recalled the masses of remote gunships drifting in space among the debris of their blasted duplicates. It had been, as Kris described, "live-action *Galaga.*"

"The CDF mopped up, salvaged the tech," Eren explained, filling everyone in on the aftermath.

A.J. noticed Lori's confusion and leaned over. "Cascadian Defense Force," he whispered. "I'll explain later."

Marc stepped forward again and gripped A.J.'s hand firmly. "You saved us. You saved our world." He took Lori's hand in the same manner, and she gave a nervous laugh.

"Hey, don't look at me. I'm new to this party." She cast a look at A.J. that told him she was duly impressed, and it made his cheeks burn red. "Didn't know I was dating a *hero,*" she gushed.

Eren pointed toward the depression where the ship was hidden. "Let's get back. There's a lot more to do."

The group trudged in the direction of the gully, and Marc continued his update.

"This morning, I happened across one of the sigils you left in the forest, and randomly arrived at the gate on this overlook. I eventually located the ship, but had to fend off what appeared to be some kind of predatory creatures that travel between portals. There were a bunch of them, but I'd picked up a sidearm from the facility. Emptied every round, then got into the ship and grabbed a weapon in case more showed up."

They descended into the shallow canyon, and Marc pointed out several dead carcasses scattered around the base of the craft. The stench was overwhelming.

"Whoa, nice shootin', Tex!" A.J. exclaimed, noting some exterior damage to the ship, but nothing as serious as a hull breach. Most of it seemed to be scratches and dings from a host of beastly claws.

"Since you've got far more practical experience here," Marc said, addressing his younger sibling, "I'll assume you're in command."

Eren grinned. "When have I ever not been in command, big brother?" Then her expression shattered. "Marc," she remembered, pausing in her tracks, "Risha's dead. We found her remains near one of the gates we left yesterday. Those creatures are not only predators, they're polymorphs. Don't let them bite you. They can assume the form of..." She trailed off, recalling the horrific discovery in Amber Scott's bedroom. "...of anyone," she finished.

Eren's brother bowed his head momentarily, then continued toward the ship. "Then we need to find Trin," he said simply. "And get the living fuck out of here."

"That's the plan," said Eren, opening the gangplank with the press of a button on her multi-key. "I've got the creatures' genetic profile. I'll feed it into the targeting computer. That should help us hit them from a safe distance. Meanwhile, I'll douse the gates while you fly."

"Sounds like a plan," Marc said, leading the way into the ship. Lori followed.

Eren caught A.J.'s arm as he and Lori brought up the rear. "You ready to do some more shooting?"

A.J. flashed a broad smile. "I thought you'd never ask."

Track 22:

WAR

Tones On Tail (1984)

Liam pulled the truck into the lot next to the Sheriff's office in Gold Beach just before 1 p.m. The place was fully staffed, with deputies heading out to calls or coming back from them, and office staff handling the regular duties of a busy Monday afternoon.

Lewis led the way, running interference with the few individuals that took note of Sheriff Chavez, who walked quietly between Chlöe and Liam with a windbreaker draped over her left arm. "Take me to my office," she ordered. "I need to make some calls."

"First call that's gonna be made," Lewis replied, "is for medical attention."

Chavez leaned against the doorjamb to her office. "You go ahead and call the medics, Lewis. I have some of my own to make."

"Who could you possibly call for help on this?" Lewis demanded, incredulous.

The sheriff pushed away from the door and, with the help of the two teens, plopped down behind her desk. "These feds thrive on darkness and secrecy," she said. "So we're gonna let some light in here."

He had no good argument to that. Nodding, Lewis shut her door and went to call the medics, while Chlöe twisted the wand to close the blinds on the office window.

Liam found a chair next to the door. "Who are you calling?" he wondered. "And how much are you going to tell them?"

"Hold that thought," said Chavez. Cradling the desk phone between her ear and right shoulder, she punched 9 on the keypad, then the speed dial for the mayor's office. This time of day, this time of week, people were usually where she could reach them. "Hello, Sarah," she chimed to the voice on the other end. "I need to talk to Bill."

She was referring to Bill Vaughn, mayor of Calico, now in his fourth term. He loved the spotlight, and any reason to gather reporters, photographers, and television cameras in one place. He was also A.J.'s uncle.

While she waited for the mayor to pick up, she winked at Liam and Chlöe. "We're gonna set us up a little press conference, and we're gonna get as much local and state media here as we can. I'm gonna get those *federales* to *vámonos*."

℞

The ship banked south above the forest canopy, causing treetops to bend and sway in its wake. Marc sat at the helm, keeping the craft as low as possible to avoid any radar the feds might be employing. He grabbed a plastic earpiece from the console and fit it over his right ear, powering it on with a touch that triggered a pulse of amber glow.

A.J. led Lori to one of four weapon stations. Brightly colored wireframe graphics whirled and coalesced on the targeting screen. A translucent plastic joystick resembling an arcade game controller glowed with neon green light, and Lori grimaced.

"I...I don't really play videogames," she admitted.

A.J. paused, tripped up momentarily by the red flag. Weighing a mental pros-and-cons list, he finally decided that this was not the deal-breaker he'd first anticipated. In the big picture, there were far more pros. "That's okay," he said, taking the station adjacent to hers. "It's pretty intuitive. You don't even have to aim. Let the computer find the targets. Just select them with the joystick, and press the *FIRE* button." He pointed out the raised red circle next to the backlit keyboard on the console.

Eren punched up a menu at her workstation, syncing her multi-key with the computer. The wireless data transfer was complete within seconds, and she slid from her chair to make her way to the hard gate in the floor of the ship, bending over the spray canister. She began to work the pump handle on the top, pressurizing the contents inside. "The targeting computer will be looking for lifeforms with the creatures' genetic profile, so you should be good to go. All you have to do is fire."

"It occurs to me," Marc said quietly, "that Trin can't use her brand to jump."

Eren scowled. "What? Why?"

"Sustained an electrical burn during the escape. She's gonna have to get to a gate in order to jump."

Eren paused, deep in thought. *Goddamn complications,* she mused. *Why can't this shit ever be easy?*

"Meanwhile, we're closing down all the local portals," Lori reminded her.

Marc turned to his sister, eyes pleading, but unwilling to give voice to any challenge.

"You guys laid the gates at Old Town," A.J. noted. "She could jump there."

It's a slim chance, Eren thought. And a slim chance was better than nothing. It was simply all they had. "Let's hope so," she said, sensing the tension radiating from her older brother.

They arrived at their destination in less than a minute.

"Approaching the first gate," Marc announced, bringing the saucer-shaped craft to hover above a clearing encircled by thick brush and timber.

The sigil below erupted with the lightning strikes of portal travel, and A.J. suddenly saw multiple targets called out on his monitor screen. "Don't jump yet," he warned Eren. "Let me get rid of these first." Using the joystick to drag across the targets, he selected a group of four, then hit the red button in front of him.

Red particle energy pulsated from the center of the craft, spiraling outward in glowing conduits to special emitters placed around the exterior. A rapid sequence of four beams blasted down to the forest floor, vaporizing the targeted creatures.

"You're clear," A.J. hailed.

Eren slung the spray canister over her shoulder and touched the brand on her arm, vanishing from the ship, only to reappear in the gate below. Extending the spray wand over the sigil in the ground, she hosed it down with the solution, watching as it sizzled and sparked like an electrical circuit shorting out.

Another predator polymorph came plunging out of the forest, bellowing an unearthly scream. Eren flinched out of instinct, but the thing was immolated in short order by a particle beam from above. Muttering quiet gratitude to A.J., she touched her scar again, blinking away to the craft hovering overhead.

☙

The girl was nineteen, dark-complected, and wore a Black Eagle flight uniform. A head of crimson-tinted raven hair was shaved in a ratty rooster crest, and her left arm bore a makeshift bandage. She crouched in the hollow of an ancient tree stump that had been carved out by lightning, environment, and time. Her arm sang with the acute pain of a third degree burn, acquired on an electric fence during their escape.

She was free of custody for the moment, which should have pleased her. But instead, she was absolutely terrified.

The portal was fresh—laid within the past day or so. That meant rescue was close at hand. But before she was able to use it, hoping to teleport to one of the gates in and around that old ghost town close to the river, more of those *things* had arrived. They clearly knew how to use portal technology. Or did they? Was it technical expertise, or instinct? Did they just sense an artificial gate as they would a natural nexus point?

Whatever the case, she knew them to be aggressive and ravenous beyond reason. One of them had savaged Risha as they ran into the deep woods earlier that morning, and Trin was still kicking herself for making a quick escape without looking back. She had no clue where she was, or how to return to the gate they'd found.

Under different circumstances, she would have enjoyed the locale. Lush...green...wild. Not unlike her own home in Cascadia. But these were not different circumstances. As it was, this place was crawling with government agents who wanted her recaptured, and trans-dimensional creatures who wanted to feed.

She realized she hadn't seen her own world in two years. A world ravaged by alien invaders. By war and famine. By plague and ecological collapse. She wondered if the CDF had sent a retrieval team to bring the weapon back, to save her world.

Maybe they had, and her Earth had been saved. Maybe it had failed, and home had fallen to the invaders. At this point, it was unlikely she'd ever find out, one way or the other. And if she was stranded here, she'd have to figure out a way to carve out a new life in this place.

Hang on, Trin, she thought. *You're not done yet. Just find a gate. Any gate.*

She cocked her head, listening to the distant sound of gunfire and animal shrieks. Sensing the coast might be clear, she dashed from the hollow.

...directly into the arms of a waiting agent.

She only struggled momentarily, realizing that her strength was best conserved for later use. As the first agent grappled her into a hold, a second approached from behind and cuffed her hands behind her back. Her left arm flared in agony beneath the bandage.

Aside from the first agent barking into his walkie talkie that they'd secured "Subject Delta", they said nothing as they walked her back to the black SUV parked on a small deer path a few hundred yards to the west.

And then everything went crazy.

The creatures were suddenly all around them, coming at the trio full force. They surged forward, all razor talons and needle teeth, growling unholy hunger, and the first agent screamed in terror as his arm was torn away at the shoulder. He collapsed onto the ground and was immediately mauled by two more dimensional terrors. The walkie talkie fell with a soft *thud* onto a carpet of moss.

The second agent reached for his shoulder holster and Trin spun away from him, snapping a lateral kick to his right knee. Bellowing in agony as his leg snapped and gave way, the agent fumbled for his sidearm, but a creature clamped its parasite maw down on the back of his skull, and he instantly went silent.

Trin was already running, leaping over ferns and trying not to fall forward with her hands cuffed behind her.

A massive shadow loomed overhead, and Trin paused, glancing up. She could see a familiar saucer silhouette through the trees, and for a brief moment, she thought rescue was imminent. Red light streamed from the particle emitters, and a moment later the creatures lay dead, blasted to piles of crisp ash.

Then the ship was gone as quickly as it had arrived, and Trin found herself again in the silent, serene forest, the mirror of her own home.

Finding the handcuff keys on the body of the second agent, she quickly freed her hands. She grabbed the radio from where the first agent had dropped it prior to having his head cracked open.

A glimmering figure beckoned from the trees beyond. Squinting into the distance, Trin recognized it as a native Coquille hunter in buckskin leggings and a fringed shirt, long hair streaming from beneath a checkered headband.

Phantoms tended to interact with people on the physical plane only under specific conditions, and they were usually restricted to travel between portals or natural nexus points. Trin theorized that this one might know where a viable gate remained, and looked as though he wanted to show her the way.

The ghostly warrior offered a final wave and turned to the east, disappearing in the dappled haze of the woods and brush.

Giving a final cautious glance around the clearing, Trin took off at a run, following the specter into the trees.

Track 23:

DON'T LET GO

Wang Chung (1984)

"Approaching target." Marc leaned on the ship controls, veering back to the west. A vast expanse of green treetops seemed to reach after the saucer as it passed overhead. They'd started with seven glyphs in the forest: the initial gate, and the six laid during their search the previous day. The gang had closed four, and Eren had just neutralized the fifth.

There were still two more gates to close, and Trin was still out there somewhere.

Radio chatter crackled in his earpiece, and Marc turned to the others. "They're sending in air support," he frowned. "Attack copters scrambling from the National Guard base in Shasta. Coast Guard Pelicans en route from Coos Bay."

"What, no fighter jets?" A.J. wondered. "I'm insulted."

"They may have limited resources to deploy on short notice," Marc said, squinting at the wireframe display in front of him. "Coast Guard copters are more for search and rescue, but the Cobras out of Shasta are pretty well armed—they could hurt us. In broad daylight, clear visibility, we're screwed if we stay out here too long."

"They're trying to trap us." Eren theorized, doing some quick calculations in her head. "It'll take the Shasta copters a good forty-five minutes to get here. I'm honestly more worried about the Pelicans. Maybe fifteen, twenty minutes. We still have a small window to get these last two closed, then back to Hanging Rock. Let's hit it."

It took less than a minute to reach the sixth gate, which was crawling with predators —countless toothy maws probing for blood. It seemed as though news of a plentiful food source had spread among the species, much like a beehive or ant colony. Once again, as the ship banked above the swaying evergreen canopy, Lori and A.J. selected targets and rained particle energy down from the sky. Eren blinked away in a flash, and returned in seconds, offering a thumbs up to Marc.

"Okay, last one," she said, moving to the navigation screen and pointing to the teens at the weapon stations. "Good work on those critters, you two."

"I think I'm getting the hang of this," Lori smiled.

That made A.J. happy. If she warmed to videogames in general, it opened up a whole new avenue of wasting time together.

Marc angled the ship in the direction of the last forest gate, just a mile away. He checked the systems monitor and pursed his lips as the screen flashed an alert in red. "Last gate was just activated," he warned.

Eren turned to him. "More creatures coming in?"

"Dunno," was the reply. "I think the targets have remained static around that gate."

A.J. pondered. "Maybe Trin got to it in time."

Bless your optimism, A.J. Eren thought. "We'll check out Old Town when we get this gate closed," she said, heading back to the sigil in the floor.

Electronic displays flashed with targets acquired, and crimson fire pelted the creatures gathered around the gate. Eren appeared in a bolt of lightning, sprayed down the glyph, and waited for it to spark and sizzle. Scanning the forest, she only registered the carcasses of a half dozen dimensional parasites. There was no other movement, no feds, no staccato gunfire echoing through the wilderness.

Closing her eyes, Eren spared some hope that Trin had found her way somewhere safe. With a caress of the scar on her wrist, she disappeared, leaving the clearing still and eerily silent.

When she arrived in the portal on the ship, Marc was already turning animatedly in his seat.

"We're getting a ping from a local source on the comms scanner," he announced. "It's the Black Eagle distress code. I think it's coming from the mine near the ghost town."

A smile of surprise crept across Eren's face. "Trin!"

"I know that spot," A.J. interjected. "I've used that gate."

Eren fixed A.J. with a solemn gaze. "Can you get her?"

A.J. winked back at her. He loved a chance to shine, especially in full view of his new crush. "Be right back." Turning in his chair, he touched the scar on his arm with a finger, vanishing with a flash.

Lori watched in amazement. Teleportation was still new to her, and she wasn't sure it would ever get old. "Damn," she muttered. "That is so killer."

☙

Trin peered beyond the stone mouth of the mine entrance, watching a couple of black SUVs making their way up Old Town Main Street. One of them pulled to a stop next to the dilapidated livery stable. Half a mile away, another vehicle was parked on the turnout overlooking the clearcut. The feds were covering the known portals, tightening the net. When the last truck arrived at the mine, she'd be steeped in agents.

She couldn't remain here.

The cavern was suddenly washed in a burst of white, and Trin averted her eyes, clamping them shut against the glare. When she opened them, a youth of fifteen stood before her in the center of the sigil burned into the rock floor. He wore glasses and casual clothes, and was otherwise so nondescript, she wouldn't have noticed him on the street.

"Trin?" the boy asked.

Moving slowly, eyes discerning, she finally queried, "Who are you?"

Part of his nerd psyche filled with a sequence from *Star Wars*, but he resisted the urge to say: *My name is Luke Skywalker—I'm here to rescue you.* A.J. extended his hand, not moving from the gate. "A friend," he said simply. "Hold onto me."

Sighing, she realized she was somewhat low on options. The feds knew about the gates in Old Town Calico, and they were presently securing them. She didn't know this person, but he was traveling the portals, and knew her name. If this was a chance to escape, she really had no other choice.

The slamming of car doors and shouting voices echoed into the cavern from outside. The agents were here.

Gripping A.J.'s hand as if arm wrestling, he brought their entwined fingers together with his left wrist, touching the portal scar.

And they were gone.

CB

As the ship returned to the overlook of Hanging Rock, Eren threw a quick look at her brother. "This is the last gate outside of Calico. If Trin didn't find her way out..."

"Do it," Marc nodded.

She took a breath, then touched her brand. Disappearing to the top of the trail head, she doused the gate, watching it sputter and steam. She blinked back to the ship, and Trin grabbed a startled Eren in a tight embrace.

"Thank you for coming back for us," she cried through the happiest tears.

Eren returned the hug, then nodded toward A.J. and Lori. "You can thank these two. And a few others."

"Thank you...uh," Trin began, at a loss for a name.

A.J. raised a half salute. "A.J. And this is Lori."

Trin smiled. "Thank you, A.J. and Lori." She moved next to the pilot's station and laid a gentle hand on Marc's shoulder. "So it's just us?"

"Just us," Marc acknowledged. "Risha is..."

"I know," Trin sighed, closing her eyes. "Then let's get out of here."

Marc turned to Eren, awaiting an official order. "We've got less than two minutes until we'll be visible to the Coast Guard. Shall I plot a course home?"

Eren nodded, approaching A.J. and Lori at their respective weapon stations. "It's time to go," she said with a hint of sadness. "The copters will sight us if we hang around. You guys should teleport back to town. When you can, close down the gates in Old Town, and at your homes."

"What about the feds?" A.J. worried.

"When we're gone, they should pack up shop again."

With a satisfied tilt of his head, A.J. stood, and Lori followed his lead.

"Are you going home? For good?" she asked tentatively.

Eren gave her a sweet smile. "Pretty much." She gathered Lori into a gentle hug. "A.J.'s a great guy," she whispered. "And he's totally in love with you. Don't break his heart, because I will *totally* come back here to kick your ass."

They both shuddered in a wave of tearful laughter.

She pulled away from Lori with misty eyes, moving to A.J. "Thank you—*again*—from the bottom of my heart." Gesturing a pause with her finger, she added suddenly, "Oh, wait." She produced a small chrome cylinder about the size of a pen light from her pocket, handing it to him. "Hit this button if you ever need me. I owe you a couple of times over."

A.J. turned the object over in his hands, examining the dormant red LED at the top. "What's this?"

"Dimensional beacon," she explained. "Our rendezvous point will be my old campsite by Rock Creek."

"Rock Creek" A.J. repeated. "You all take care of yourselves." He pulled Eren into a tight hug.

Eren didn't want to break contact, but she knew their time was limited. Aircraft were inbound. "You guys better go," she warned, holding A.J. by the shoulders. She nodded toward Lori and added with a sly grin, "Take care of each other."

Marc punched up a travel route on the nav screen. "System's not letting me plot the nexus point north of the river."

"Oh, we closed that one," A.J. said matter-of-factly. "Too many phantoms."

Marc stared blankly back at him.

"There's another one over Mt. Shasta," A.J. offered.

Casting a glance at Eren, Marc sputtered, "How does he...?"

"Plot the Shasta nexus point for our exit," Eren confirmed. "I'll catch you up when we're out of here."

A.J. offered his hand to Lori, and she took it. "Your ride, miss," he said with a smirk.

"Safe travels," Lori managed to say before the two vanished in a blast of air and light.

CR

Two black SUVs and a matching Ford sedan pulled up in front of the Curry County Sheriff's office, remaining at the periphery of the throng of local and regional media, public officials, and curious citizens.

Sheriff Linda Chavez stood on the front steps of the square building, neck and shoulder expertly dressed in fresh bandages courtesy of the medics from Curry General. She held a manila folder under her arm, and was flanked by Deputy Lewis, Calico Mayor Bill Vaughn, and Dr. Bollinger, with Liam and Chlöe standing close by.

Liam fidgeted nervously in front of the banks of cameras and microphones aimed in their direction. At least he wasn't their sole focus, and the sheriff had given them explicit instructions regarding what to say—or more importantly, what *not* to say. With any luck, the press wouldn't be asking a lot from the minors on hand.

Chlöe leaned close and whispered something to Liam. She'd seen the feds arrive, and he nodded in silent acknowledgment. As the two teens watched, Chavez addressed the gathered crowd, holding the folder in full view.

"This is a file of alleged 'evidence' of wrong-doing by Deputy Pete Halverson," she began, "sent to us not long ago by an unnamed federal agency. Alleged wrongdoing which led to Deputy Halverson's apparent suicide. In the course of our investigation, we determined that much of the so-called evidence had been manufactured, as this department can verify Deputy Halverson's whereabouts. I was personally on calls with Halverson during times this 'evidence' claimed he was out of state."

Chavez looked at Deputy Lewis, who offered a nod of encouragement. She turned back to the gathered reporters and local Gold Beach and Calico residents. "We believe this manufactured evidence was in reprisal to our ongoing investigation of Project Black Eagle."

Glancing at the agents standing beside their parked vehicles, she noticed the exchange of panicked looks as she said the last three words.

"While we don't know the specifics of this top secret government project, we have discovered that the agency involved has been operating out of a secret facility in the Siskiyou National Forest since at least 1982. They were willing to manufacture evidence to pressure a loyal Curry County sheriff's deputy to halt his investigation, and when he wouldn't back down, they had him assassinated."

A collective murmur of astonishment spread through the crowd. She'd used the term "assassinated" on purpose, and it had the desired effect. One of the agents pressed a finger to his earpiece, listening intently.

"We also have recorded instances of this agency tampering with evidence in several recent local deaths," Lewis added, watching as Dr. Bollinger nodded agreement. If he feared for his job or his life, he certainly wasn't letting on.

"Whoever is behind Project Black Eagle," Chavez warned, "should know that the Curry County Sheriff's Department serves the public trust, first and foremost. We are here to protect the residents of this county and will not be bullied."

The agents suddenly climbed into their cars and began to pull away from the parking lot.

Chavez had one last thing to add. "After internal investigation, Deputy Pete Halverson has been cleared of all allegations of wrongdoing, and Project Black Eagle is on notice. We are aware of their activities in and around Curry County, and have notified state and local authorities to be on alert. We see them. They may have us outgunned, but we can make things very messy for them if they try to push us around."

The locals in the crowd roared approval, as the reporters pressed in with questions, and Chavez and Lewis took turns fielding them like champs. Mayor Vaughn muscled his way down the steps, adding his own praise for Sheriff Chavez and her department in keeping the town of Calico a safe and desirable place to live.

The Reynolds family station wagon arrived, Kris at the wheel. He negotiated around the gathered crowd, pulling into a space in the back lot, where Liam had parked the El Camino.

Liam and Chlöe ducked away, skirting the corner of the building toward their arriving friends.

"Well," Liam said, taking a deep breath and letting out a huge sigh, "let's hope the feds take the hint."

Chlöe smiled. "Time will tell."

Kris and Molly stepped out of the wagon and assembled with the other two by Liam's truck. There were relieved greetings all around.

"Any word from Eren?" Molly wondered.

Liam shook his head. "Not to my knowledge. If she finished the mission and got home, we might not hear from her again."

"That'd be sad," Kris added. "I've missed having her around."

"True story," Molly agreed.

There was a flash from the truck bed, and the group turned to see A.J. and Lori standing in the middle of the sigil. It looked as though they hadn't been seen by the spectators at the front of the Sheriff's office.

A.J. did a quick head count to see they were all present and accounted for, then smiled at his friends.

"What did we miss?"

Track 24:
THE PARTY'S OVER
Talk Talk (1982)

Summer settled over the Rogue River Valley like a worn blanket, threadbare but familiar. While that familiarity was adequate for most, Liam found that as time wore on, he focused more on the threadbare aspect. His life now bore the tatters of tragedy beyond his years. His mother was gone, and though his house was modest, it now seemed far too big, as he was now kicking around inside it alone.

A week after the press conference, Sheriff Chavez collected the gang together for a debriefing, taking copious, detailed notes. A.J. tried to convince the sheriff that Eren had in fact rescued the recovery team—those who'd survived, anyway—and would probably not be returning any time soon, if at all. If past experience was any indication, the agents of Project Black Eagle had likely packed up shop yet again.

Chavez and Lewis supervised the return to Old Town Calico, and Liam hosed down the sigils in the mine, the livery stable, and in the turnout near the road. The group met privately to discuss the fate of the sigils at each home, with some arguing to keep them intact, and others warning of the appearance of the dimensional parasites. Liam insisted they all be shut down, and that was that. But before they finished with the portals at home, Liam and A.J. took a quick jump to the sigil in the Project Black Eagle site in the Siskiyou forest.

They found it deserted. Again.

Spraying down the portal with their vinegar solution, they watched the glowing shape spark and sputter. Then they teleported back to town, closing the portals at each house, and in the back of Liam's truck. With those gates closed, the only active sigil remaining was the one at the Rock Creek campsite. Liam told the group he'd be responsible for shutting it down.

A.J. eventually revealed the beacon Eren had given him before their escape. He told the group what she'd told him: that she owed them, and would come back if they ever needed her. So although they missed her off-the-charts charisma in their lives, she wasn't totally absent in theory. At some point, if the situation required, they could call in a favor. Kris argued that it was really *two* favors.

The summer gradually fell back into a somewhat functional routine. Bodhi returned from Europe and found that his backpacking adventures couldn't hold a candle to the stories he was hearing. He was disappointed to have missed Eren, but tickled to see A.J. in his first romantic relationship.

A.J. went back to his part time shifts at the Val-U-Drug. Kris continued waiting and busing tables at his parents' diner. When Molly wasn't hanging out with Kris or the gang, she spent her days journaling. Bodhi and Chlöe made several trips up the coast, camping on the dunes in Florence, and making out on the Old Town overlook. She ended up taking a job at Dave's Deli, and Bodhi filled what remained of his summer break working on a beat-up 1972 VW Super Beetle he'd purchased for two-hundred bucks from a surfer in Crescent City.

Lori got a part-time job at the art supply store in Gold Beach, but was otherwise ever-present around Calico, shooting her black-and-white photos and sketching whatever grabbed her fancy. She and A.J. were inseparable, going to movies and the occasional concert (when a decent band would stop in Portland or Eugene).

The group went to Brookings to watch *The Karate Kid*, and there was some discussion over pizza at Gizmo's that they should make the Cobra Kai skeleton costumes the group Halloween project. A.J. prevailed in his argument that the Cobra Kai dudes were colossal douchebags, and the *Ghostbusters* concept was much better from any angle. No one could disagree with that logic.

In July, they went in pairs to see *The Last Starfighter*, and later spent hours discussing the similarities between the plot and their experience fighting the space invaders in Eren's dimension. Of course, A.J. just assumed the feds had their homes bugged, and someone had leaked the idea to a Hollywood screenwriter.

Later that month, A.J. and Lori began collaborating on a 'zine showcasing A.J.'s fiction and Lori's poetry and photography. A.J. photocopied them after hours at the drug store, and the Silver City Diner sold them for fifty cents each.

By the end of July, the group tallied up exactly zero phantoms and the same number of mysterious agents prowling the area. It looked very much like Liam's theory had born out: with Eren gone and the local portals closed, the feds had packed up shop—and the specters with them.

The release of *Red Dawn* was another source of group bonding and knowing looks across buckets of popcorn in the darkened theater. How many times had they felt like the Wolverines, besieged on all sides while trekking through the ferns and conifers of the Rogue River-Siskiyou National Forest?

The answer, upon reflection, was *one time*, really. But once had been quite enough.

Liam grew ever more distant as the summer wore on. He spent fewer evenings socializing with the gang, remaining holed up in an empty house or on his favorite spit of sand on the river, smoking weed and gazing at the stars. He kept hearing Sheriff Chavez in his head, repeating the words she'd said to him the night she brought his mother home drunk.

One way or another, life will move on.

When the heat spiked in late August, they gathered on the river at their party spot to celebrate A.J.'s birthday and driver's license. They listened to the mix tape artistry of Lori and Molly, and made plans for the coming school year. Molly would be a sophomore, Chlöe a senior, and the rest would become juniors. They posed for a group photo, taking advantage of the timer on Lori's camera.

Lori wandered among her new friends, snapping shots with her Nikon, preserving the moment. Life was moving faster for them. They were growing up. And they each wanted to make the time they had together last as long as possible.

It was then that Liam revealed he'd activated the beacon the previous night at A.J.'s, returning it to the drawer in his friend's desk before he noticed.

Their look of collective shock was enough to break his heart. "I've been kicking this around for weeks," he tried to explain. "I'm going away."

A.J. was gobsmacked. "Going away? Like with Eren? To her Earth?"

Liam stared at the ground. "You guys have a lot going for you. I can't really say the same."

"Dude," A.J. protested. "What the hell are you talking about?"

Liam folded his arms defiantly. There was no changing his mind. "My mom's dead. I have no family left. I've looked at my probable future if I stay, and it ain't pretty. I'm not going to college. I don't have any prospects except working as a grease monkey for the rest of my life, and hanging out with you losers until you get tired of my shit." He'd intended to soften the insult with a bit of levity, but it fell flat. He hung his head and sighed. "Probably end up a drunk...like *her*." Everyone instinctively knew he referred to his mother.

Molly approached, worming her way past his folded arms into a hug. "Don't say that. You choose your path, not anyone else. You're our bro. We'll always be here for you, and we'll never get tired of your shit, I promise."

"Oh, I guarantee you *will*," he maintained. "I'll just end up holding you back. All of you."

Kris screwed his face into a mask of complete incredulity. "Fuck that noise. You're not gonna hold us back, man."

The group crowded in, hugging Liam in turn. What had started as an intended farewell among friends was quickly becoming an intervention.

"Dude, you have a house and a car," A.J. reminded his friend. "That's not a bad start. You're almost seventeen. You can file for legal emancipation. I know Chavez would help you."

Liam smiled suddenly, breaking away from the arms around him. "Speaking of which..." He walked to his backpack, which was sitting open on the picnic table. Producing two envelopes, he handed one to A.J., and one to Molly. A.J. opened his to discover the pink slip to the El Camino. The car Eren had rebuilt and gifted to Liam on her departure was now being passed to him.

"Congrats on the license, dude," Liam said, clapping A.J. on the shoulder. He nodded at the unopened envelope in Molly's hands. "I'm all squared away on the house," he explained. "My mom didn't have a will, but Chavez helped get through probate without a hitch. It's been paid for since '78, deed is now in my name. Your folks' real estate office can sell it, take the commission, and distribute the proceeds between the group. Probably get close to fifty grand for the place. Get a start on the old college fund."

"Does she know?" A.J. asked.

Liam shrugged. "Chavez? I told her I was going back to Montana with Eren. She probably suspects, but didn't say anything. If you get the chance, tell her goodbye for me. Tell her...tell her I'll be okay."

They stood together in the afternoon glow of the sun sparkling on the river. There was a long pause, then Kris broke the silence. "You...you're really gonna do this?"

"Yeah," A.J. answered for him, the realization sinking in. "Yeah, he's gonna do this. And we're gonna let him, because he's our friend, and we love him."

Liam fought back what tears he could, though some escaped. He faced the group with a forced smile. "I love you guys too. Take care of each other."

A.J. and Lori smiled in unison, remembering those very words Eren said the last time they'd seen her.

Then Liam touched the scar on the inside of his arm, and vanished in the summer air.

Realizing he'd kept the gate at Rock Creek open for this exit, A.J. and the rest of the group piled into the El Camino and the Reynolds family wagon, and headed up Highway 515 to Eren's secret spot, which she had told A.J. would be their rendezvous point if she was ever summoned back.

At the campsite, A.J. found Liam's weed sprayer on the ground, and a snapshot thumbtacked to a tree. It was a picture of himself with the gang, taken at one of their their cookouts in the summer of '83—Eren surrounded by her adopted family. He recalled it had been taken by Sheriff Chavez on Molly's Instamatic, and that Eren had taken the print with her. By leaving it, she was letting them know that she'd been here, and that she loved them all very much. He smiled, beginning to feel a bit jealous of Liam taking the reins and seizing his newfound independence. What would it be like to go live in a place that had been ravaged by war, huge populations depleted, where Eren said they were regarded as heroes?

A.J. started to see the appeal. Liam would be known, of course. But more importantly, he'd be useful.

They found nothing else but the sigil, smoldering in the late afternoon sun. Liam had finally closed the portal, as promised.

Six friends stood together, smelling the pine and ozone on the summer breeze. Kris and Molly held onto each other in silent reverence. Chlöe gripped Bodhi's hand like a vice, wiping tears from her cheeks. A.J. stood from kneeling over the deactivated gate, wrapping an arm around Lori's hip. It felt natural.

"Good luck, man," he said softly toward the golden sky. Through the grief of losing one of his best friends, there glimmered a sunbeam of happiness for Liam. He had a singular opportunity to carve out a whole new life somewhere—an entirely new existence, in an entirely new reality. And he knew that Eren would guide and protect him.

Lori leaned in, planting a firm kiss in the crook of his neck. "This could be a good premise for a story," she whispered.

"Oh trust me," he replied. "I know. Eren suggested it a year ago."

They wandered back to the cars, and A.J. slid the photo print into the metal clip on the sun visor. They drove back to town along the lonely wooded highway in silence. But it was not silence of an awkward variety. It was silence born of security in each other, of shared experience, and the imagining of their lives ahead.

No matter where their individual paths led them in the future, all of them would forever share the adventure that was the summer of 1984. A moment etched in time.

Finally, A.J. pushed in the mix tape Liam had left in the stereo, cranking the volume as Blue Oyster Cult's *Burnin' For You* erupted from the speakers.

Lori cracked a smile. This wasn't her taste in music—*dino-rock*, she called it—but she could appreciate it for the place it held in Liam's heart. In A.J.'s heart.

A.J. reached over to entwine his fingers with hers. It had been one hell of a summer. But they had their whole lives yet to live, and he was absolutely thrilled to do at least some of it with the goth goddess from AP Lit. And his hometown friends.

Time to get to it, he thought.

The End

ABOUT THE AUTHOR

Todd Downing's love affair with genre story-telling dates back to his consumption of classic radio dramas and comic books as a child in the 1970s, which broadened into a general appreciation for sci-fi and fantasy media of all kinds.

He grew up in the greater San Francisco Bay Area, writing and drawing from a young age, his works ever-present in school literary journals and newspapers, and eventually on film. He married his high school sweetheart and moved to Seattle in 1991 where he began to write professionally, and worked as an artist in the videogame industry until his publishing company became a full-time operation, while raising two children amid the chaos.

Downing is the primary author and designer of over fifty roleplaying titles, including *Arrowflight, Grimmworld, Airship Daedalus*, and the official *Red Dwarf* RPG. He continues to write genre fiction for stage, film, comics, audio, and adventure gaming products.

Widowed to cancer in 2005, Downing remarried in 2009 and currently enjoys a mostly empty nest in Port Orchard, Washington, with his wife, her mother, and a rotating roster of rescue cats. Fortunately, he has an office with a door that closes.

OTHER WORKS

Calico Kids

The Parish

Sakuru

Primordial Soup Kitchen
A Collection of Short Strangeness

Airship Daedalus series:

Book 1: *A Shield Against the Darkness*

Book 2: *Assassins of the Lost Kingdom*
(by E.J. Blaine)

Book 3: *The Golden City*

Book 4: *Legend of the Savage Isle*

Book 5: *The Arctic Menace*

Book 6: *Raiders of the Red Storm*

Plus:

AEGIS Tales
A Retro-Pulp Anthology, Volumes 1 & 2

AVAILABLE NOW
in ebook and print!

Join the author's mailing list:
www.todddowning.com